SOLD TO THE WEREWOLF

A WOLF SHIFTER BIKER ROMANTIC SUSPENSE

SUMMER COOPER

Copyright © Lovy Books Ltd, 2017

Summer Cooper has asserted her right under the Copyright, Designs and Patents Act 1988 to be identified as the author of this work.

This book is a work of fiction. Names and characters are the product of the author's imagination and any resemblance to actual persons, living or dead, is entirely coincidental.

In no way is it legal to reproduce, duplicate, or transmit any part of this document in either electronic means or in printed format. Recording of this publication is strictly prohibited and any storage of this document is not allowed unless with written permission from the publisher. All rights reserved.

Respective authors own all copyrights not held by the publisher.

Lovy Books Ltd
20-22 Wenlock Road
London N1 7GU

ISBN-13: 978-1548756550
ISBN-10: 1548756555

1

Jane Sanders was fresh out of college, in debt up to her eyeballs and eager to see what the world had to offer a mere week ago. Now stood at the graveside of her parents, her mind blank, numb, as tears rolled down her face. This was not how her new life was supposed to have gone. Looking down at her younger brother, Jane's brain kicked into gear as she realized she was now responsible for the child. An adorable brown-haired little boy of eleven years old with the cutest freckles smattering his nose stared glumly at the coffins saturated by the Louisiana spring rains despite the marquee. Their parents were dead. They were now orphans.

Jane heard the priest saying words, making

sounds, but all she truly heard was the sound of the rain pelting on the plastic tent covering them. She only saw the drops of water sliding down the sides of her parent's caskets, caskets she had no clue how to pay for. There was insurance money, she knew that, but someone else had taken care of the arrangements. She and Charlie had just picked things out and then gone home, shocked to their very core.

She'd been on her way back to Ruby Bayou, a storm heading her way, when her mother had phoned her. She'd plugged her phone into her car stereo to talk hands free and the sound of the phone ringing had made her jump. Her mother had been on the other end of the line, telling her daughter to be careful because the roads were starting to flood. Jane was driving west just past New Orleans. On the highway the roads were fine she'd started to tell her mother when she heard a scream and the most awful sounds of metal being crushed and tires squealing in protest. Jane hadn't known it then but her parents had just been crushed to death by a tractor's trailer whose load of cut cypress had come loose and swung into her parents' car.

Jane listened to the screaming, tortured

sounds of her parents in the car as she pulled off to the side of the road. She'd screamed at her mother, begging her to answer. After a few deathly quiet moments Jane heard a sound from the other end.

She wasn't sure but she thought she'd heard her mother speak once more before a strangled breath was suddenly cut off.

"Jane." A pitiful sound, garbled and full of pain but Jane would swear to the day she died that her mother had called out for her. The paramedics that soon came swore there was no way Jane could have heard that sound, her mother's head had been all but decapitated by a cypress log but Jane knew she heard her mother calling out to her. She just knew it.

She knew what that one word had been. It had been a plea, a final request for Jane to take care of her brother. Jane put her hand on the little boy's shoulders as he began to sob and vowed to do whatever it took to provide for him and to give him everything he needed. She didn't know how she was going to do it but she would, somehow.

As the caskets were lowered and the gathered mourners said their farewells to Jane she hoped there was enough left from the life insurance money to tide them over until she could get a job. She'd been coming home, coming back to start her life as an adult with a degree and a weighty student debt. Her plans of staying with her parents until she'd found a job and a place of her own now crushed.

Jane drove Charlie back to her parents rented home and put him to bed, the little boy turning down her offer of food or company. He just wanted to be alone. Jane had no idea how to comfort him or what would help him and so she let him go to his dark room while she looked around the house her parents rented. A modest shotgun house, the rent was reasonable on two incomes but Jane knew she couldn't afford it. They had a couple of weeks left; hopefully the insurance money would come before then.

Soaking in the tub later, trying to hide her sobs with the sound of running water, Jane let the grief overwhelm her. It almost choked her, stealing her breath away it was so fierce. She was the grownup now, there wasn't anyone to comfort her, and she couldn't let Charlie hear her. Her family were all very religious, her mom's sister and her father's brother, along with all of the aunts and uncles. Jane's parents had distanced themselves from the rest of the family.

All of Jane's friends had either moved away for school or had new spouses and children. Jane was alone, truly alone, and so she cried in the bathtub, alone. Pulling her knees to her chest to have something to hang on to the young woman let her pain out until the tub was full, then brushed her tears away and quieted her sobs. Time to be a big girl.

Two weeks later, fifty-three job applications, and one meeting with her parents' attorney, Jane felt desperation settling in. There was no money and no job on the horizon.

"What do you mean there's nothing, Mr. Templet?" Jane almost shrieked. "There has to be something, they both had insurance policies."

"Yes, but with the bills they owed and the cost of the funerals, there's simply nothing left. In fact, there's a balance of $1,542 at the bank on a loan they took out." Alton Templet, the lawyer, an older balding man with thick glasses and a nasally voice in an ugly brown suit, looked down at the papers rather than at Jane.

"A balance. And what happens if I don't pay that loan? It's not in mine or Charlie's name."

"Nothing really. They can't come after you two for it and the car was totaled in the accident. You will eventually get a sum from the company that operated the tractor and the company that hired them to transport that load but it may be a couple of years. They may settle quickly, the evidence is clear that that load wasn't tied down properly and that driver was cited for many violations. We can hope they settle quickly but they may not."

Jane, her waist length black hair twisted on top her head, dressed in a severe black suit with black heels, tried to hold back the tears. So she'd have money but it could be years from now. She wrung the tissue in her hands to shreds, her tender skin turning red as she did so.

"And what about the house? The landlord sent me an eviction notice. He wants to sell the house apparently." Her voice shook, her world in a perpetual state of collapse now.

"If you can't pay the rent then there's nothing

I can do. Do you have friends you can stay with until you can find a job?"

"No, not anyone I'd want to impose on." Jane shook her head as she spoke. They'd all help her any way they could, one had a fundraising campaign going online now but Jane needed a lot of money. She had her student loans coming up soon, a child to take care of and a car payment to make, on top of rent and groceries, insurance, and all the rest of the stuff that goes with being a responsible adult.

Alton Templet, a man leaving middle age behind, looked over at the girl with sympathy. Thirty years ago he might have offered the beautiful young woman with almost yellow eyes and a lovely face some advice about how to make some quick money. Not in today's world though. He bit his tongue and held his hands out helplessly.

"Perhaps you should see if there's someone more suitable to care for your brother?" He asked tentatively.

Jane's head snapped up and her eyes shot angrily to the lawyer. "No. Charlie's my brother; he's not being taken from me."

"Of course, Miss Sanders. I was only trying to

help. Charlie will need stability, care, and attention. I'm sure you'll find a way." The lawyer looked away from the young woman, not wanting to rile her.

Jane shifted; her slightly plump frame filling the tiny uncomfortable chair that might look good in a magazine but wasn't practical for actually sitting in. Jane's hands felt the satin smoothness of the wood and hated it. Keeping up appearances was important to Jane but not if it caused discomfort to others. She shifted once more and decided it was time to leave.

"Well, please keep me informed about the settlement or whatever is happening with the companies that caused my parents' deaths." Jane's voice broke on the last word. She was holding on to the anger for now and not screaming that her parents were basically murdered but her grief was still breaking through on occasion. "Excuse me. As I said, keep me informed please. Good afternoon, Mr. Templet."

Jane shook the man's hand then left. When she arrived home her friend Dodie greeted her at the door. Dodie had set up the online fundraising campaign and had also organized a bake sale this coming weekend. It was one of the reasons Jane loved her hometown, people came together to help out in any way they could. Ruby Bayou may not be a huge town, with less than a thousand residents, but it was close and community-oriented.

"How did it go?" Dodie asked, pouring a cup of coffee from the pot she'd made earlier, for Jane.

Jane sat at the table with her friend and took the coffee gratefully. "Not well. Thanks for sticking around waiting for Charlie to get home from school."

"No problem, honey. Anything I can do."

"I don't know what I'd do without you!" Jane gasped as her tears started to flow once more.

"Come now, Cher, stop that crying. We got this." Dodie encouraged, taking Jane's hand.

"I don't know how we'll do it. The rent is due next week, we're almost out of groceries, and nobody wants to hire a new graduate. I've even gone into other parishes looking for work. I guess accounting isn't necessary around here." Jane hiccupped through her words, wiping her eyes with a tissue Dodie had given her.

"We got you babe. I swear. One way or another." Dodie promised, squeezing Jane's hand.

Jane went to sleep that night, her friend's reassurances helping her rest finally. She'd spent the evening helping Charlie with his homework and fixing him dinner. A simple chicken Etouffee with rice, which was the boy's favorite. Charlie bathed and sat up with her to watch his favorite science fiction show, cuddled up at her side.

Charlie wasn't doing a lot of talking about his emotions but he clung to his sister when they were alone. He was at that age where he was testing his independence anyway but now he felt like he had to be a man for his sister. He knew what had happened, he understood that his parents were gone, and he missed them terribly but he also wanted to be a big boy for his sister. She needed him, he thought, and he was trying very hard.

Jane heard his light snores when he fell asleep and looked down. Charlie's sweet face, with the same smooth olive skin as her own, was angelic in sleep. Jane felt a tug at her heart and put her arm over the boy. Something had to give soon, it just had too.

A week later Jane learned that fate can

always deal you one more blow. The property owner showed up with the police to evict her and Charlie.

"But I have the rent you wanted. You said if I could raise $800 we could stay, I have it." All of the joy she'd felt when Dodie had given her the $1300 from the bake sale disappeared in an instant. She could pay the utilities and the rent until she found a job of some kind, any kind.

"Well, that's not what we agreed. You agreed to $1500 not $800, missy." The tall, overweight man in a stained tank top and a handlebar moustache said before he spit chewing tobacco juice at her feet.

Feeling panic rising, along with the urge to vomit, Jane looked to the sheriff for help.

"You can't pay, you gotta go Miss Jane. It's that simple." The man hung his head in shame.

Jane thought he should hang it even lower. Her thoughts were actually all over the place.

"So we have to get out now? Charlie's still at school!" She declared. "His bus will bring him here!"

"You'll have to go pick him up or something. I can give you enough time to clear the place out but then you have to go, Miss Jane." The sheriff said, holding his arm out to the property owner.

"You know he's lying right? None of that was in the agreement." Jane said, anger starting to win out finally. "Our parents just died and he's kicking us out and lying in order to do it. You're a pig!"

Jane spat at the property owners feet then went back into the house with the sheriff. She called Dodie and Dodie promised to bring over a truck and a trailer. Jane had the $800 for the rent that was going to have to go on a storage shed and whatever she could find for the night.

"I got you a place, it's not much, but it'll work for now. And it's close to me. My brothers will be here in five minutes. You go pick up Charlie, let us take care of this until then." Dodie pushed Jane out of the door and went to work.

When Jane came back there were women and men moving around boxing up goods and carrying it all out to cars, trucks, and vans waiting outside. Within an hour the house was empty. Jane stood back shocked.

"Wow, Dodie. That was incredible!" Jane had never seen a house emptied so quickly. "What's this place you've got for us?"

"It's not the best place in the world, but it's close to me and it's clean." Dodie looked doubtful for a moment but then perked up. "It's just temporary, until you can get something better. Or you can come stay with me."

"Oh, I don't want to impose. Lead the way please." Charlie got back into the car with Jane, his little eyes round and shocked. Jane worried this might be a little too much for the little boy.

"It's alright Charlie. We can do this honey." Jane said, trying to convince herself as well.

"We can, sis." He said, his tone cheerful all of a sudden. "I'm okay, promise."

"I hope so Charlie. I'm sorry I'm such a horrible sister." She said, tears evident in her voice.

"You are not! You're trying so hard, sis, you really are. You can only do what you can do."

Jane spared him a glance, amazed at how wise her little brother was. He'd been a surprise, but she'd loved him from the start. She'd do anything for him and had felt that way from the moment he'd been born.

"You know I love you, kiddo?" She said with a smile, her gaze going back to the road.

"I love you, sis! Where do you think we're going?" He asked, curiosity winning out.

"I don't know but if it has a roof I guess we should feel lucky." She stared ahead, hoping for more than a roof. Just a little more than a roof.

2

Jane and Dodie sat in the front of her trailer, a cheap table and umbrella protecting them from the sun, and watched Charlie climbing onto the bus. A trailer, she was living in a trailer. With her little brother. Jane wanted to hang her head in shame.

"You know, when I was little I always dreamed about having one of those houses on the right side of the Bayou. One of those giant contraptions on stilts made of cypress with lots of windows. I'd marry a blonde god, with a compassionate nature, a partner, who supported me in all things as we produced the requisite number of children and went to church functions or something. You know, that cookie cutter life that the women on this side dream about but never quite comes true?" She looked over at Dodie as she sipped her coffee.

"I know, Cher. Some of us get it on this side, we manage to cross over the Bayou, but not all of us. I won't be going to that side any time soon." Dodie was a lesbian, which wasn't a problem, but there weren't many in our small town. She'd avoided college and worked as a care assistant for an elderly man. She was good at her job and planned to go to nursing school but hadn't done so yet. She insisted she'd give Mr. Cavalier her time until it was his time then she'd go to school.

"I don't know what to do. Apparently I've wasted my time with this degree. I only have a few more months then I have to start paying back those loans I took out." Jane mused. "I'm just going to have to take whatever comes along. That $800 is gone now."

"There's always welfare, Cher." Dodie advised, not looking at Jane.

"I'm going to get what I can for Charlie, at least the medical part. I don't know about the rest of it. I don't know if I could ever walk out the door again if I had to get welfare." Jane had her pride, after all.

"Honey, you think some of those women on

that side of the Bayou don't go shopping until it's late so their friends won't see their EBT cards? It's part of life now, sometimes you got to take the hand that's offered you, like it or not." Dodie said sternly but with care. "Welfare isn't nothing to be ashamed of, as long as you don't make it a way of life. You need help, take it."

Jane agreed but it still stung. She'd grown up poor, with that stigma. Even though they'd worn school uniforms, the kids had still somehow known her uniforms were either secondhand or cheap. Jane couldn't tell the difference but the other kids could. She didn't want that for Charlie.

"Maybe something will turn up soon." Jane said, going back in for more coffee. "You got us a place to live, after all, that's our own."

Jane saw Dodie smile as she took the other woman's coffee cup to refill it. The trailer was old, probably early 80s, Jane still didn't know, and had a smell of old carpet and cigarettes long since burned away. The walls were still standing though and the plumbing worked. Best of all, it was only $200 a month and sat on a private lot. She didn't have nosy neighbors or a nagging landlord to deal with. The property owner was a friend of Dodie's that lived in the northern part of Louisiana now. Jane just sent the money to them online and that was that.

Now she just needed a job. The online fundraiser had only raised enough to keep Jane and Charlie fed. Jane guessed orphaned children, especially when one of them was grown, just didn't raise much interest now. She took the cups back outside after refilling them and sat down next to Dodie.

"There is one place I know of. It's a little rough, a biker bar, but a friend of mine works over there and she comes home with stacks of money." Dodie finally said after a long silence.

"A bar? Would that mean I have to dress like a tramp and show my tits to strange men?" Jane quipped jokingly.

"Oh no, you dress however you want to and you have to take the upper hand with those people. But you'd make enough for the bills." Dodie said, not looking at her friend.

"Where is it?" Jane finally asked after her own silence.

"I'll take you over at lunchtime if you want."

"I have to, don't I? If nothing else it will tide us over until I can find something I won't have to get groped at." Jane sighed deeply and put her pride away. It was for Charlie.

Jane got the job and started working that same night. Charlie went over to Dodie's house, the two planned a night of video games and car racing movies. Jane was just glad to have someone she trusted to take care of her little brother while she worked. Dodie worked in the mornings usually and she'd insisted on keeping Charlie for nothing. Jane couldn't beat that deal but planned on offering her friend a nice dinner when she could afford to take her out.

Jane pulled into the gravel driveway of the worn down building with plywood over the windows. It was a little ways out of town and most people didn't even know it existed. The paint on the wooden structure looked as though one too many hurricanes had passed without it being repainted and Jane wasn't sure but she thought the building had been white. A small sign over the top of the door proclaimed it to be Tommy T's Place but other than that there was no light, no beer signs, or anything else to give it away as a bar. Only a long line of motorcycles and pickup trucks gave away the fact that people were inside the place. The thumping sound of music was also a clue but not many paid attention to it.

Jane took a deep breath, reminding herself that Charlie was at home, in need of new shoes for gym class, and they were low on groceries. She told herself this was only temporary, not forever. Taking one more deep breath she took the key out of the engine and opened the door.

Jane got out of her car and slung her handbag over her shoulder. Pulling her cutoff denim shorts a little lower on her thighs she wished she'd worn something besides the black tank top she had on. She'd tried to dress to match the women she'd seen in the bar but this wasn't normal attire. This is what she'd wear to fishing or something. You couldn't show up to a bar in a suit, though, could you, she told herself.

Squaring her shoulders, her long hair loose around her shoulders, Jane walked into the place and flinched as the powerful speakers blasted her with a deep bass of a classic rock song. She knew she was going to need something for a headache within the hour. She looked around the place as the door closed behind her. Burly, bearded men in black leather played pool at the six tables setup on one side of the bar, others sat at tables talking or at the bar staring into their drinks quietly. Jane saw the man that had hired her earlier that day and walked behind the bar.

"Right, until you get your license, which is needed in the state of Louisiana to serve liquor, you're just going to have to watch. We'll send you tomorrow for that license. Tonight, just watch and you can take orders to the kitchen." The bar served a few snacks, nothing complicated, and Tony, the owner, gave her the menu.

"Look that over for now, learn what we have, what we don't have, and watch." Tony, a man well over six feet tall with light brown skin and gentle brown eyes, should have been scary but he wasn't, he was rather gentle in fact. He'd handed her the menu and Jane looked it over as instructed. "Any questions?"

"Yeah, why's it called Tommy's if your name is Tony?" Jane asked, a perplexed look making her beautiful heart shaped face look cuter than it already was.

"Beautiful and observant!" Tony cried with a

laugh. "Tommy was my dad, I inherited the bar from him."

"Oh, cool!" Jane said as she shook her head. "That's great!"

Tony went off to take an order and Jane spent the night taking orders for drinks and food. None of the men bothered her but they tipped well and Jane was trying not to go digging in her pockets to count her tips when a tall man walked in that caught her attention. In fact, everyone in the bar turned to look at him before going back to whatever they were doing, but at a quieter level.

"Who's he?" Jane asked Tony as the owner walked by for a beer in another cooler.

"That's Zare. Leave him to me tonight." Tony said looking put out.

"Alright." Jane agreed but watched the man.

Powerfully built with long black hair pulled back into a bun, the man had a powerful physique that his tight t-shirt and jeans displayed perfectly. He was a handsome fellow whose mere presence drew your attention. Black motorcycle boots made his steps heavy and Jane could have sworn she felt the steps in the floor as he went to an empty table, a vibration that went straight up her legs to places best not thought about. Jane couldn't look away from the man and as he sat down his gaze caught Jane's.

Were his eyes black? Holy shit! Jane took a step back, the powerful man exuding something that drew Jane to him, even though he was far from the type of man she'd want. Her blonde god or a poetic Shelly type with curly light brown hair and sensitive eyes. Nope this mountain of manmeat was hard, his eyes even harder. She wanted the kind of guy this man ate for lunch. She looked away, telling herself he wasn't for her. But something intrigued her and she kept catching herself looking at him throughout the night. Jane watched as the few women in the bar flocked around the man and Jane tried not to feel a spark of jealousy when he invited some of them to sit down with him over the coming days.

He never invited her to sit with him, only gave his order and went back to whatever he'd been doing. That was fine with Jane, she was afraid of saying something stupid to the incredibly sexy man anyway. The days turned into a week and Jane was left on her own at last, a license in hand and a book with recipes on the bar. She'd gone from dropping orders and bottles to a fairly decent waitress over the first days and was learning how to deal with the patrons of the bar as the bartender. Jane did a lot of observing in the first couple of weeks, keeping her head down and not making any waves with anyone, including the other staff members. She saw some of the other women disappearing in the back with a man every now and then, only to come back with the man adjusting his pants. Jane didn't ask, she knew what was going on.

Her observations showed her this wasn't a place she wanted to still be working at a year from now. Zare might be sexy as sin and filling her dreams at night but he wasn't the kind of man she wanted. He was the head of a biker gang, for goodness sake! Jane felt out of place with him, with the other brash and brazen bar staff. She wasn't loud, she wasn't overtly sexual, she was just herself, and that often meant quiet.

She brought home enough in tips to keep her and Charlie going but she'd still signed him up for Louisiana's version of Medicaid and they lived on a thin wire between being broke and not being broke. That's when fate stepped in again to kick Jane in the teeth once more.

Her car had been giving her problems for the

last few days now and when she left work that evening it wouldn't start at all. Business hadn't been so great that night and now her car wouldn't start. Her tips would pay the rent but that was it, there was no money for a tow or car repairs, or even to call someone out to see if a jump would start the damned car. She'd call Dodie but that meant getting Charlie out and it was after one in the morning. She hung her head on the steering wheel, her arms cushioning her face and tried not to cry as a tap came at her window.

She looked up to see Zare standing there.

"Need some help?"

That's when a desperate plan formed in her brain, a plan to keep her and Charlie ticking over. She gave an inviting smile and rolled the window down.

"I think I might. My car won't start and I'm all but broke. You wouldn't happen to know anything about cars would you?" She asked, leaving the smile in place.

"Oh, a thing or two yeah, Cher. Crank it, let's see what it's doing."

She turned the key and nothing happened at all. It didn't even click.

"Ah, your battery is dead, Cher. That's not going to be a cheap replacement." He looked pained for a moment.

I'd sworn I wasn't going to do this, that I was above this, but I knew where this was headed and I didn't step away. Part of that was just plain old attraction, some of it was curiosity, but a lot of it was desperation. Jane stepped out of the car, letting Zare get a good look down the slinky top she had on, a silky red number cut low.

"I don't suppose you could help me out?" She asked, letting her hand reach out to trail down his chest.

He looked stunned for a moment, then for a fleeting moment disappointed, before his face went back to its usual blank mask.

"I think I might, you got a place in mind?" He asked, his voice stony.

Jane stepped back, learning against the car.

"Have you?" Her nerves made her voice shake but she held her head high, defying her own fear and the emotions she tried not to identify as shame as he took her hand.

3

He led her to the back of the bar, to a porch where the bar held barbecues on the long summer weekends, to an outdoor couch with cushions. Jane looked around and saw there was nobody around, they were totally alone. She wanted to back out, she wanted to run to the road and just start walking home, trusting that the money would show up somewhere, but part of her wanted to do this.

A part of her that had never taken a real risk in high school or college wanted her to finally break free and do something just for herself. Jane didn't know if she was just trying to convince herself to do this or not but suddenly she wanted to be naked with this man and do some of the things she'd experimented with in college. She'd had sex before, but never like this, never so brazenly or for money. She'd had sex with her college boyfriend, furtive couplings in her dorm room late at night, but not very often and not very satisfactorily. He'd said she wasn't very good at it and she believed him. Now she was about to do it for money, she decided she'd try some of the things she'd seen in some of the adult movies she'd snuck and watched late at night.

Jane felt her hand, warm in his, and chewed at her bottom lip for a moment. What was she about to do? Her sanity tried to return for a moment but she smothered it down, focusing on his full lips instead. They were almost hidden in his neatly trimmed beard and moustache, but she could see them when he talked or smile. A lush red color and smooth looking, his lips had drawn her attention a lot too.

Zare sat her on the couch and sat down beside of her. She felt him beside of her but had no idea what to say to him. What do you say to a man you're about to fuck for money? Nice night?

She took a deep breath and Zare must have guessed she had no clue what she was doing because he pulled her around, pulling her to his chest as his lips came down to hers. It wasn't a rough movement, it was actually quite romantic in a way, and Jane smiled, relief filling her. He wasn't going to be rough with her.

She felt her pulse skyrocket when his lips grazed hers, the rough hair of his moustache and beard tickling her face as she sought out his lips. Then they were together and she inhaled deeply, smelling the scotch he'd been drinking earlier on his breath. It gave her a warm feeling that soon pooled low in her stomach. Jane finished twisting and straddled the man, leaning down to kiss him once more.

He was a very good kisser, tantalizing her with his teasing tongue as his hands went up to her waist, to the flirty black and red skirt she wore. It barely covered her bottom but Dodie had insisted it would bring her more tips. That hadn't worked tonight but she had a feeling the two dollars she'd paid for it in a charity shop would turn out to be a good investment.

"I've been watching this skirt all night, floating around that pert ass of yours. I was hoping you'd bend over and flash me your panties but you didn't." He rasped out before he pressed his lips back to hers.

Jane felt a power in that moment, a control she hadn't felt before. He'd wanted to see her panties, watched her all night waiting for it. She felt a sexual thrill knowing that and giggled. Her giggle turned into a moan, however, when he thrust up between her thighs, his erection pressing into her. Oh that wasn't playing at all.

Jane pressed down into him and moved back to look into his eyes. They were black. She thought maybe they were just dark brown or blue but they were actually black. She could see the orbs clearly in the moonlight. She'd never seen black eyes before but his were beautiful depths of hidden emotions. Jane let her body take over then and stopped thinking, determined to make the most of this.

She leaned back, pressing her barely covered breasts into his face. She wasn't a tiny girl and her breasts matched her body. Zare stared at her for a heartbeat and then his large hands moved up her back and around to cup her globes. His thumbs stroked over the area where her nipples were and she felt his touch even through the padding that hid her nipples from view.

Jane felt her back arch even more and longed to feel his lips on the tight tips, wondering if his facial hair would tickle or arouse her even more. She soon found out as he undid the buttons of the top and moved the cups of her black bra out of the way. Zare pushed her breasts together and used his tongue to moisten the tips before sucking both into his mouth. She felt his straight white teeth scraping the buds and Jane moaned loudly, a bolt of pleasure zinging right down to the dark area between her legs.

She felt Zare thrust up into her heat once more, and thought she'd explode there and then. Fifteen minutes ago she'd had no idea this is where she would be but she wouldn't change where she was for anything. There was a magnetism about the man, something that drew her and made her want to throw caution to the wind. He'd barely started to touch her and she was already near something she'd never experienced with a man before. On her own but never with a man.

Jane rotated her hips, pressing into Zare as he dragged his lips across her nipples, pulling them taut before letting them go. Jane moaned in protest but he went right back to them, his teeth rasping at the tender flesh once more. She wasn't sure which was better, his teeth scraping her nipples or his lips sucking them. She didn't care particularly; she was just enjoying riding the hard length of flesh pressing into her tender flesh below.

Zare started to suckle at her once more, his lips and teeth working together, and Jane's breaths soon turned into pants as she writhed on him. Her breath stopped when she heard a deep growl low in his chest, a sound of satisfaction and pride, an encouragement that tipped her over the edge of sanity and deep into a place of pulsing pleasure and strokes of red lights.

She held on to Zare's shoulders as her body convulsed, her pleasure unlike anything she'd ever felt before. She ignored the throbbing red light as some weird manifestation of squeezing her eyes shut, unimportant when she was coming so hard, she felt as though her body was turning inside out.

ZARE STARED UP INTO THE YOUNGER WOMAN'S face. He knew she was young but old enough to work in a bar so old enough for sex. He'd watched her over the days, going from a fumbling newbie to a more in control bartender and waitress. She'd caught his eye, not just because she was beautiful but because she seemed so innocent. She didn't seem like the kind of girl who'd come to work in a place like this bar. She belonged in some lawyer's office, not behind a bar.

He'd developed a soft spot for the quiet woman and a fascination with her. All those times she thought he hadn't seen her watching him he'd known. He'd felt her gaze and a part of him had yearned for her. But she wasn't the rough and tumble kind he was used to. Maybe she was exactly what he needed at the moment.

When he'd seen her in her car on the verge of tears he'd wanted to help her. Her face when she'd looked out at him had torn at his heart. She was such a good girl, she avoided the alcohol on hand, she side-stepped the pills and drugs offered to her, and he'd never once seen her going in the back with a man as the other women did. She was a good girl, she didn't belong here. That didn't stop him from wanting her in his bed.

When she'd made her offer Zare had felt disappointment, a pain in his chest, but he wasn't about to turn the opportunity down. She'd filled his dreams, even when he'd taken another woman home with him, and he wasn't going to pass up what she offered. Part of him told him to turn it down, to just give her the money he could easily afford to give away, but he couldn't. He needed to touch her. To taste her.

Now she was coming apart in his arms and he watched as a red mist flowed from his skin to hers, marking her invisibly with his stamp. Zare watched, fascinated as his wolf claimed the girl, the woman, in his arms. He didn't know this could happen but he knew what it was. He was a wolf shifter after all, weird shit happened. And his wolf had just claimed a woman. Whether he'd planned it or not, she was in fact what he'd been looking for.

Zare kept his thoughts to himself, as usual, letting the woman in his arms have her moment of pleasure. He ached to be inside of her though and wondered if she'd let him. He didn't have a condom with him. He knew he couldn't give her anything, he was a wolf shifter, they were immune to human diseases, but she didn't know that.

He could feel her moist heat even through

the denim of his jeans and her panties. He let his head fall back as her sighs and moans turned to heavy breathing and her body stopped vibrating in his arms. The night was cool but a fine sheen of sweat gleamed on her skin as his hands rubbed down her back, soothing her as she came down.

Then she moved, kneeling up to pull at his jeans, tugging down the zipper as she pushed at his pants. His cock sprang free, hard and thick, the long length pulsing in her hand. Zare's gaze flew to her face, a question in his eyes as she sank down onto him, ignoring his face. Her moan of pleasure as deep, guttural, something he'd not heard from a woman before. She'd truly given herself over to this moment.

Zare stopped thinking when he felt her bare labia opening for him, the panties somehow disappearing as she sank slickly down his shaft. He'd wanted her desperately, dreamed about her, wanted to know what she'd feel like clamped around him. The reality was far better than the fantasy. They moved together and quickly Jane was pulsing around him once more, her inner muscles milking him hard as she came apart in his arms once more. Zare let his own restraint go and joined her, the silken moist heat of her pussy far too much pleasure to ignore.

Zare gave a short shout as his body exploded, his cock pulsing inside of Jane as his fluids left his body, filling her deep and hard. Jane's body was still pulsing around him, her cries peaking once more as he filled her and Zare knew this was not going to be the last time, even if she did ask for money.

He held her as their bodies calmed, kissing her hair and her face as her breathing evened out. He offered to drive her home if she was ready to go and she accepted. She didn't ask for a dime as she got off of the bike and walked into the house, a slight wobble to her knees. Zare smiled a smile of pride and happiness. She'd do just fine.

JANE WOKE THE NEXT MORNING IN A DAZE. SHE hadn't been able to ask him for money, the experience had just been too good to ruin with dirty talk of money. She'd find a way, even if she had to walk to work. She needn't have worried because her car was in her driveway when she got up, the keys in the seat. She went out with a huge smile on her face and found the car started right up. Zare had taken care of it then. She hid her smile as she went back into the house. She didn't know what any of this meant but she kind of liked it. Even if Zare wasn't the yuppie she'd always dreamed of.

Jane told herself not to jump the gun as she looked down at the single red rose she'd found in the passenger seat and walked through her home to wake up Charlie. She was still in a haze of happiness as she sat on the little boy's bed and stroked his hair to wake him gently. He was covered from head to toe with a light blue comforter and Jane leaned down to kiss his head as he came awake.

"Come on, little brother. Time to wake up." She teased him, laughing as he pushed her away. Then he groaned. "What's the matter lovey?"

"I don't feel good, sis. I really don't." He stayed on his side, facing the wall. Charlie was getting to that age where fake tummy aches came along with a more independent nature but this morning Charlie didn't push her away and he wasn't the type to fake being ill, he liked school and being with his friends. Especially since their parents died, he'd been really good about going to school without complaint.

Jane reached down to his forehead and finally noticed how warm he felt. She sat up in the bed, concern her most immediate response.

"What else is wrong, Charlie?" She asked, not sure what to do for him yet. Maybe he just had a bug?

"My arm hurts. It hurts real bad." He said pitifully.

"Can you sit up for me?" She prompted, still stroking his hair.

She saw his cheeks were rosy but his short sleeved pajama top didn't reveal why his arm was hurting. She couldn't see anything but Charlie wasn't a complainer. He was ill if he said he was ill. She hugged him then told him to get dressed and she'd take him to see the doctor. Jane was very glad in that moment that she'd signed him up for LA Chip and that Zare had fixed her car.

She drove him in to the doctor, Jane's own pediatrician, who took one look at the child and told her to get him to the hospital.

"But what's wrong with him?" She asked, panicking.

"I don't know for sure but let's just eliminate

a few things. I can't do the tests here but they can at the hospital. I'll call ahead and get it arranged. Go on now, take him on over." The doctor, a gentle, knowledgeable man, set her at east but Jane still worried. What was wrong with Charlie?

4

Jane sat in the hospital room with Charlie, his little fingers tapping at the screen of her phone as he played a game. She couldn't get the image of his little body, covered in countless bruises, out of her mind. Charlie couldn't tell her where the bruises came from but they horrified her, especially the ones on his back. Then there were all of the little red dots on his arms and chest. What had caused all of that? At last a doctor came in and sat down to talk to Charlie.

"So, little fella, can you tell me anything about these bruises and what's going on with you?" The red headed woman asked. She was very pleasant and Jane and Charlie liked her immediately. "I'm Dr. Evans, I'll be looking after you for a while. You can talk to me."

Charlie grinned at her. "You're very pretty."

"Oh, a charmer already." She winked at Jane then went back to Charlie. "About these bruises?"

"I don't know they just showed up the other day. I keep getting more. And my elbow hurts. I don't feel real good either, I'm tired." He said, going back to his game.

"Alright. We're going to take some of your blood out of the IV Charlie and we might have to keep you here for a few days. I promise lots of ice cream and your own remote to the TV. How does that sound?"

"Awesome! Can Jane have ice cream too? She works so hard, she deserves buckets-full!" Charlie asked, excited and not caring about grammar.

"Sure she can. I'm going to send in a nurse to get the blood and talk to your sister outside for a minute. Just hit your buzzer if you need anything."

Jane followed the doctor out, her smile immediately disappearing as she saw the doctor's face.

"What's wrong?" Jane cried.

"I think Charlie is very ill Jane. He's almost certainly got leukemia, we just need to find out for sure and determine what kind. He needs you to be strong. I've read your story in the paper and I know you've been strong already but your brother is going to need a lot of strength, Jane. A lot." The doctor held her hand out as Jane's knees wobbled.

"And those bruises? What's so important about those?" Jane latched onto the question to bring her back from the urge to faint.

"Those are typical of the disease. That's what has me almost convinced, those bruises. Let us get started on these tests and we'll see how it goes. I'll be back as soon as I know something concrete. Maybe before then." Dr. Evans squeezed Jane's elbow before walking away.

Charlie was brave, even saying how cool it was to watch his blood fill the tubes. Jane watched him, the now familiar numb state keeping her from falling apart. Charlie knew something was up and tried to be brave for Jane. He made a game out of everything and kept teasing Jane to make her smile. But the little boy knew something was wrong, he could see it in her eyes, the tears she was trying so hard not to shed. He finally lay down to nap, his own worry sapping what little strength he had left.

Jane watched him sleep then went out to call work and Dodie. She also went to the ladies room to cry in peace, letting the sobs tear through her once more. Alone in a bathroom, crying once more, Jane sobbed out her pain and fear to the unresponsive walls.

Jane finally pulled herself together and went to check on Charlie. Dodie was there waiting for her and she took Jane into her arms. Dodie wasn't a huge woman but she was fluffy and Jane felt as though she was being embraced by a pillow. Of an even height, the two women were built similarly, but Dodie was prettier, Jane thought. Dodie let Jane have a moment then pulled her out of the room.

"Let's get you fed, then we can talk, Cher. Come on." Dodie could see the absolute terror on Jane's face and knew it was bad. Whatever was wrong with Charlie was very bad.

Hospital food was never pleasant but Jane couldn't taste it, she only ate to keep Dodie off of her case. Once she'd finished the foam cup of tea and polished off some gumbo with a toasted cheese sandwich Dodie finally let her speak.

"They think it's leukemia." Jane put it bluntly, leaving no room for quibbling about perhaps it was something else.

Dodie swore then covered her mouth, looking around in embarrassment at the people that had looked over at her. She took Jane's hand and squeezed it. That earned more disapproving looks from the elderly women at a table across from them so Dodie dropped Jane's hand and sighed loudly. She wasn't good at this acting "normal" gig, that's why she usually stayed to herself. People were far too judgmental for her taste.

"What do we do then?" She finally asked, sitting on her hands and clamping her lips shut.

"We wait for the doctor to come back, for now. She's fairly certain of the diagnosis. Then we plan the attack I guess. Isn't that what they do with cancer, attack it?" Jane's hands fluttered over the table, as if to show how lost she was.

They went back up to Charlie's room and settled in for a long wait. Jane dozed for a little while and Dodie stepped out to go get both of them some food once the sun went down.

Charlie had woken up and asked for a milkshake from a fast food restaurant and Aunt Dodie was going to give him whatever he asked for. She knew what Jane would want so she left her to rest.

They were all eating when the doctor finally came in with the test results. She looked far too grim for Jane's liking.

She sat on Charlie's bed, by his feet and looked at them all. Then she looked at Charlie.

"Charlie, do you know what cancer is?" She asked quietly.

"Yes. Sort of. I've heard the grownups talking about it and seen it on TV and stuff. I don't know what it does but I know it can make you real sick." He looked at the doctor with fear in his eyes. Jane's heart broke when his voice started to shake and she went to sit beside him on the bed.

Dodie went to the other side of Charlie's bed and sat with him, her admiration for the boy growing as he took the news far better than either she or his sister did.

"What you have is called leukemia, it's a cancer of your blood system to put it simply. The organs that make your blood and bone marrow are sick and that makes you sick, in turn. If we don't stop it the sickness is only going to get worse. We'll do all we can to stop it though Charlie. Do you have any questions?" Dr. Evans looked at all three people sat on the bed with her.

Jane was too stunned, Dodie wasn't sure what to ask, but Charlie had one question that needed answering.

"Am I going to die? We just lost our parents. I can't leave Jane on her own. I just can't. You have to fix me Doctor." Charlie reached desperately at the doctor, his fear overwhelming him. It was fear for his sister, though, not for himself.

"We'll do all we can to stop that, Charlie. I promise." The doctor turned her head away quickly but Jane caught the sheen of tears in the woman's eyes.

His doctor had compassion at least. Jane had no idea how this was all going to work but she'd learned a lot since her parents had died. Fate wasn't kind but people could be. Dodie was a rock she knew she could depend on. Taking a deep breath she asked her own question.

"Will he have to stay in the hospital?" She hoped his Medicaid would cover all of this.

"For a while yes. And when we start treatment he'll be in a ward where we can control the environment." Dr. Evans told her.

"Right." Jane took a deep breath, feeling like she was sinking under a wave of grief, worry, and fear. She looked over at Dodie and knew she wouldn't be alone, not totally but what was she to do?

Jane desperately wished her parents were still alive, still there to make all of the decisions she was having to make, and to be here for Charlie. Jane was exhausted and felt like her energy had been drained away before she'd even built up a supply.

"Look this is always a big shock, even when it is suspected. We aren't going to have an exact plan in place for a few hours. I suggest we start with transferring Charlie to the children's ward, get him settled in, and then we can talk about everything. You won't be able to think of questions for a while and I'll be around any time, just have me paged." The doctor left with a reassuring smile.

Jane didn't feel as though the woman had been rude, just sensible and she appreciated that. She needed sensible right now. For a moment her cheeks flamed as she remembered her night with Zare. No, she probably shouldn't be making decisions at the moment, not after that fiasco but she was all Charlie had. Time to buck up and be a hero, for Charlie.

From that point on Jane's life became visiting Charlie in the hospital, calling doctors and nurses, working, and working on fundraisers. Charlie's insurance covered some of his care but there were things Medicaid refused to pay for. If there was a cheaper way, even if the outcome was less positive, then they would only pay for the cheaper alternative. She still had to pay for a lot of Charlie's medicines, the non-medical items he needed, and the bills at home. Through all of this Jane continued to work.

She kept her head down, staying in her own private world at work. A world where she set out the things she had to do the next day while dealing with groping customers and trays full of drinks. She didn't let her work ethic slip, she just disengaged from what was happening. She didn't talk to Zare over the next month, nothing more than the trivialities you had to discuss with customers.

Her boss and the other girls knew what was going on and supported her as much as they could, switching shifts when she needed it and letting her pick up extra shifts when she could. Jane was grateful for the help but her world was fading away in the hospital. Charlie's treatments had destroyed his immune system and he was fading away. He even looked like a ghost sometimes. His brown hair was gone, his pink healthy skin had turned almost translucent, and his eyes were just voids.

He never complained though. Jane was proud of how brave he was being and they spent many nights talking about what they'd do when he was better. Jane promised she'd do whatever it took to make him better. But the medicine wasn't working; she could see it in the doctor's eyes and Charlie's face. He was getting worse, not better.

"Jane! Phone call!" Patty, one of the waitresses called out to Jane as she brought back a tray full of empty shot glasses.

Jane felt her heart fall to her feet and ran to the phone. It could only be about Charlie, nobody else would call her at work.

"Hello?" She breathed into the phone, suddenly panting in fear.

"Jane, we need you here. Please come right

away." The doctor's voice shook as she spoke and Jane's nerves screamed a little more.

"What's wrong?" She demanded to know, needing something.

"One of his lines got an infection and turned septic. We've put him in a coma to give his body a chance to fight the infection. He's not doing well."

"I'll be there in ten minutes." Jane hung up the phone, told Patty what was wrong, endured the wasted moments for a hug, and ran out to her car. She pleaded with fate, God, whoever might be listening to let Charlie still be breathing when she got to the hospital.

"What can I get you, Zare?" Patty looked up at the very tall man that always made her shiver. She might be an older woman but she could still appreciate a fine looking man and Zare was one of the finest.

"What's up with Jane?" He asked, settling at a barstool.

"Interested, Cher?" The woman asked, handing over a glass of his usual scotch.

"Maybe. What's going on?" He took the glass, sipping the fiery liquid. He enjoyed the burn as Patty started talking.

"Her kid brother is sick, Cher, cancer. Has it real bad. He's in a coma now, got some kind of infection or something so they put him under to help him fight it."

"Damn." He stated simply. It was all he had to say.

"Yeah. It's bad for her and that little boy. Their parents just died, now this. She'd got it rough, yeah, a lot rougher than some of these other women in here selling their souls for a pill. She's a good girl that Jane. You could do worse." Patty looked over at Zare with a deep look, telling him far more than he'd asked. Her amber eyes fell as Zare looked into them and she turned to another customer.

"Yeah, Jane is a good girl." Zare finished his drink and went out of the bar. He was meeting some of his clan tonight, they had a shipment coming in from Texas and they'd all be heading out in the boats soon enough. He needed to know more about Jane first though.

He sent out a call for one of his clan to find out which hospital the boy was in and when they called back with the room number he started his bike and headed over. This couldn't wait. He'd let his second in command take over for the night.

Zare found the floor and quietly walked to the little boy's room. He looked in to see Charlie, pale and lifeless in the bed, Jane weeping over his hands. Both of the boys hands were taped up, IV lines running to several bags on each side of his bed. Damn, that poor kid, he thought to himself as he watched quietly from the doorway. And so unnecessary.

Zare knew what he had to do then.

5

Jane rested in one of those uncomfortable hospital chairs that they refer to as a convertible bed. Jane was certain the designer snickered as they created it, possibly thinking they could sell it to a BDSM club as a torture device if the hospitals didn't buy it. It had been a week and Charlie was still fighting. The infection was improving but the cancer refused to budge, much like this chair the hospital staff insisted doubled as a bed.

She stared at her little brother, made tinier by his battle, and wondered what happened next. The doctor said he needed some new kind of treatment and the insurance wouldn't cover it because it was too expensive. The insurance people said it was too experimental but they all knew it was just too expensive and when you're poor you don't get to make decisions about your own healthcare.

Jane tried to hold back a sob, knowing there was little she could do. Her one foray into getting paid had gone really, really well but she'd not been able to take money for the experience. She'd only been able to do that because she'd been watching Zare, fighting her attraction to him, and had finally given in. She couldn't do *that* with men for money, not men she didn't know. Jane shuddered and put her fist in her mouth to hold back the tears.

Dodie walked in and hugged her friend when Jane stood.

"Anything?" Dodie asked, her voice quiet and calm. Her eyes held a sliver of hope but that was crushed when Jane shook her head.

"No, and the insurance won't pay for anything other than what he's getting now."

"We'll find a way." Dodie promised, taking Jane's place in the seat. "Go home, get a shower, get a nap, and then go to work. I'm here for the day. Amy's coming later to take my place, and then you can come after work. I know you will."

Jane gave her friend a grateful smile and picked up her things. She went to Charlie, running a finger down his cheek before she left. She didn't want to touch him too much, not when his immune system was so compromised. She made sure the nurses knew she was leaving and that Amy was on the visitors list, then went out into the warm afternoon air. She paused for a moment, inhaling deeply to calm her nerves before she drove home.

After a shower and a power nap Jane headed into work, her mind on autopilot once more. She had to pull her shorts down as she slid out of her car seat and wondered how long she'd wear this kind of "uniform" before she found a job that required her brain, not her ass, for the money she earned.

Pushing through the front doors she felt the thumping bass of the music like a wall that she'd become used to bumping into. Looking around she knew it was going to be a good night for tips. There were two different pool leagues in the bar that night and Zare was playing on his team already.

The man turned out to be a master pool player, well known throughout the state for his skills on a table. Jane watched him for a moment as he stretched out over the table, his fingers placed delicately on the table. She knew how dexterous those fingers were and she remembered how they'd played over her body. Her cheeks flamed and, as though her thoughts had prodded him, he looked up into her eyes, heat instantly filling their depths.

Jane inhaled sharply, her heartbeat suddenly racing as he gave her a slow wink and took his shot. Jane heard the ball fall into its pocket but didn't see it. His gaze had pinned her in place. Jane could suddenly hear the song pounding into her ears and thought, yeah, she needed him now, most definitely. To forget her fears, her worry, her sadness for just ten minutes would be great.

Zare stood up and broke the spell though and Jane chided herself. It wasn't that she wanted to forget Charlie, she thought as she went into the back and dumped her stuff in a closet, it was that she wanted to forget the pain for a moment. She had taken on the role of mother and Charlie was her world but she desperately needed a moment without pain. She watched some of the other women in the place and knew there was other ways to numb herself but didn't want those ways. She'd be fine, she told herself, as she put on an apron that only covered her hips, and walked out behind the bar.

"I'm so glad you're here!" Patty called out, pouring up several shots at once. "It's insane!"

Jane grinned at the older woman and went to work, taking drink orders, passing out bottles, and taking payments. She lost herself in the mad dash of bartending and was soon in a zone of her own. She helped Patty catch up then went out to take food orders. Four hours later Jane was still in her own zone but struggling to stay there. Four hours of ignoring offers of sex for drugs, skirting tables and customers, dodging groping palms aimed at her bottom, and appeasing increasingly drunk customers was taking its toll. She was heading back to the bar, the floor slick with spilled drinks and who knew what else when someone moved unexpectedly and she dropped an entire tray full of shot glasses when she swerved to miss them.

"Oh shit, sorry Cher!" The drunk man garbled out. "Let me help you."

He bent over, spilling his entire beer over her head and down her shirt. Jane jumped back from her crouched position and shrieked as the cold liquid soaked her. She fell back, her hand finding a shard of glass and she screamed again.

"Patty!" Jane heard Zare calling as he came to her. He picked her up from the floor and pulled her up in his arms, carrying her to the backroom.

Jane saw some of the regulars dash to clean up the glass and Patty came out with a broom. Jane hid her face in Zare's shoulder and held her hand out, blood dripping down her slashed palm.

"That's pretty nasty, darlin', let's have a look at it." Zare said as he sat her down in a chair.

Jane was holding back the tears, fighting to keep them behind her eyelids, but one slipped through. When Zare reached up from where he knelt in front of her and wiped it away with a gentle murmur Jane lost it. She sobbed, holding her hands out as she bent at the waist. She knew the people out in the bar could probably hear her, even over the noise in that area, but she didn't care. She couldn't be strong anymore.

Zare watched Jane as she let go of her tears and his heart melted. Sure, he needed a wife to appease his clan, but he'd chosen Jane for a reason to begin with, she was strong, capable, the kind of partner he wanted in life. She wasn't sitting around waiting on someone to take care of her; she went out and did it herself. Knowing she needed someone to care for her and she was still so tough, she'd cracked.

"Let me help you, Jane." He murmured to her as he stroked her back, soothing her with his touch.

"Oh, it just needs some bandages, my hand will be fine." She said as she sat up, wiping at her face with a towel he handed her. "I'll be fine, really."

He placed another towel around her hand, staunching the blood for now and smiled.

"I didn't mean that. I have an offer to make you. It will take you away from here, from this life of struggle."

"Oh, you're my genie in a bottle are you?" Jane scoffed with a grin of her own.

"Not quite a genie, no, but I can help. Let me talk to Patty then we'll bandage your hand up and get you out of here for the night." He stood but Jane called him back.

"Don't! I need the money. I can't lose a few hours wages, I can't." She said desperately.

"I'll pay you those hours, plus some. Come ride with me." He smiled at her for a moment, his heart thumping in his chest as she decided. He was surprised he actually felt apprehension over what she'd decide.

Zare watched her thoughts flicking over her face, her indecision, her denial, and then a smile as she clearly decided that she needed a moment of her own.

"Alright, genie, let's see what you got!" Jane had made a decision; she hoped it wouldn't cost her the job.

Zare knew she needed a break, a moment to herself without the stresses of her day and hoped giving her a ride on his bike would help her when he dropped the bomb in her lap that he was about to unload on her.

He ran in to let Patty know he was taking Jane home, came back in and wrapped some gauze and bandages around her hand, noting the cut wasn't very deep, and pulled her by her other hand out to the parking lot. He felt his phone vibrating as he handed her a helmet and checked it to see that the shipment had been moved out to the Bayou behind his house, all in code of course, and smiled happily.

Business was going to plan and Jane was going for a ride with him. He'd been confused when she didn't even acknowledge his presence the day after their tryst but a talk with Patty had revealed the problem. He'd bided his time, hoping she'd turn to him but she'd stood strong on her own until tonight. He had a plan, he wasn't sure it was the best plan in the world, but he was hoping it would work.

Zare helped Jane get the helmet on when he realized the bandages were keeping her from closing her hand properly, the cut in her palm making the bandage awkward, and fought the urge to lean down and kiss her. She was cute but tempting in his helmet, her face smiling up at him as her head wobbled until she became used to the weight.

"I've never been on one of these before." She revealed, and he felt his heart melt again.

"You're going to love this. I promise." He

pecked her on the nose to appease his burning urges and helped her get on.

He climbed on himself and started the bike. He heard her gasp as the engine came to life with a loud roar and a vibrating purr.

"All you have to do is hang on and go with the tilt of the bike. Don't get jumpy or lean in too much, but don't fight the urge to lean a little. You'll get the hang of it quickly." Zare told her as he put his own helmet on. He settled down onto the bike and went to work. It was time to make Jane fall in love with the bike.

JANE LET HER HANDS SETTLE AT HIS WAIST AND SHE felt how very powerful he was even though his clothes. Lean muscle and flesh met the touch of her hands and her thighs. She'd never been so intimately close to a person while being driven around and it was a novel sensation. As he drove them into the darkness of unlit streets, the warm air rushing over and around them, Jane felt herself begin to relax.

She'd been thinking about that night she'd spent with him since he offered to take her out of the bar, and when she'd felt the vibration of the bike a pleased responding purr had started in her chest. But as the ride went on she settled in, and let the drone of the engine and Zare's reassuring presence lull her into a quiet place.

Jane had worried that she'd turn into some kind of horny monster on the back of the bike but instead she fell into a place where she had thoughts but they didn't matter. She was one with the bike, with Zare, and with the wind. She'd found a peaceful place where nothing could intrude and she clung to Zare as she let her troubles melt away for the moment. She'd feel guilty if she could but in that moment, with only a single headlamp to light their way, she was in her own world and she could be selfish for a little while.

Jane felt her brain clearing and her body relax, her breathing slowing down, and her heart rate settling down to a normal pace she hadn't felt since she'd first taken Charlie to the doctor. This was peace and she understood now why so many people fell in love with this lifestyle. She was free for the moment, for the time that the wheels thrummed on the road and the engine roared through the night.

Jane was surprised when they pulled up to her house and she realized they'd been riding for an hour. And Zare was speaking words at her as soon as he turned the engine off. She knew because she could feel his chest rumbling but the words just didn't register. She snuggled into him some more, her arms wrapping more tightly around his waist.

She heard him chuckle before he stepped away. Zare helped her down from the bike and Jane pulled him over onto her garden swing. A gift from a friend the swing had almost become her refuge when she came home from work. She'd often swing in it for a bit before she went inside. She was still buzzing from the ride and she wasn't ready to go in yet. Here under the moon reality still couldn't intrude and Zare might kiss her.

She rested her head against his shoulder and this time when he started to speak the words finally made sense. As the words sank in she sat up and gaped at Zare.

"You want me to marry you? What the hell for?" She asked, staring at him in shocked amazement.

"For my own reasons, I need a wife. Quickly.

You need money to take care of your brother. I wouldn't make any demands of you but that you always maintain the integrity of who we are, who I am, and my family. No flagrant affairs, no bad behavior, just stay who you are and make sure the world believes you are my wife. I'd like us to actually make an attempt at a real marriage but your plate is rather full at the moment."

"I'm so lost." Jane said, sitting up on the swing, forcing the motion to stop suddenly.

"I need a wife Jane. I'm willing to pay whatever it takes to give your brother what he needs and to take care of you both for the rest of your lives in return for your loyalty and promise to always act as my true wife in the public eye." He wasn't meeting her eyes but she could see he was nervous in the way his booted feet tapped on the ground and his hands kept going up to run through his hair.

"No, you can't be serious, Zare. That's ridiculous. People don't participate in marriages of convenience anymore, it just...oh my, I can't believe this." She stood and started to pace around the small yard.

"I am very serious Jane. Look, think about it. I'll have it all drawn up in a pre-nup. if you want.

Give me a call when you've thought about it and let me know. I'll have your car brought over later. I'm going to go and let you think on it. But please, do think about it Jane. I know it sounds like a joke but I would never joke about this. Too much is at stake. Call me, alright? Even if it's to say no." Zare bent down to kiss her cheek, sending sparks through Jane's cheek, before he hopped on his bike and drove away.

Jane stared after him, wondering what had just happened and if she'd gone insane somehow. Marrying Zare, and all of his money if rumors were to be believed, would take away all of her problems. But what was she getting herself into, marrying a man like that? She'd heard the rumors about drugs, about the criminal aspects of Zare's "business", and about the bike gang. But if he really had all of that money he could afford Charlie's treatment. And Charlie meant everything to her. She was willing to sell herself if Zare was serious and it meant saving Charlie. She knew she didn't need time to think and pulled out her phone as she went into her home, scrolling through her contact list until she found Zare's number.

"Hey, it's me. Call me when you get this." He

was still on the bike, obviously. She had a little time though and waited patiently, pondering what she was about to do. It could either be the biggest mistake of her life, or the answer to her prayers.

6

*J*ane shifted in the hard chair, staring at the pictures on the wall of the elegant restaurant Zare brought her too. Tasteful black and white pictures of life in the Bayou decorated the dark wood walls. Jane had never been in a place where tasteful decorations adorned the walls. Plastic sea life and shrimp-nets maybe, but never dim lighting, candles, and artistic pictures. Was this what he had to offer her? An elegant life interspersed with rough and rowdy fun?

She could feel her pulse rising as she thought about what she was doing and looked at the man she'd just agreed to marry. He was handsome, if broody, and very dark. His hair was black, even his eyes were black, his skin tanned to a golden brown. His eyes came up to meet hers and she felt her desires rising as his already dark eyes somehow became even darker, his arousal obvious in the way he gazed at her. He looked hungry.

"Ahem. Well, Zare." She stumbled to a halt, unsure of what to say now that she'd agreed to be his wife. He'd bowed his head and gave her a simple thank you. But what else did she expect? His undying gratitude? She was the one that was gaining the most here, not him. "Um, so why do you need a wife?"

Jane's eyes widened as the question came out before she could stop it. It didn't really matter to her but it did, somehow it did matter.

"My clan. You'll understand later, after we're married. I can't reveal much to you at the moment but after we're married I'll tell you anything you want to know. I'm the head of our group, not just the bikers, but the clan, our family. I really can't go into it at the moment but I will soon enough. They want me to marry, I will marry."

"Right, that didn't really help. But I guess it

doesn't matter, so long as I'm not breaking the law." She gave a confused smile and took a sip of her wine. Was she breaking the law by not marrying for love? What was the law on marriage anyway?

"There's nothing illegal about it, I'm not marrying you to avoid jail or anything along those lines, I'm just trying to appease my clan. Now, what about the wedding? The clan will demand a party at the very least, we can do that at my house, I have the room and the setting for that, but do you want a civil or religious wedding?"

"Civil, I'm not religious at all. I, um, well, who's paying for it all? All of my money goes to bills and Charlie's care." Jane's cheeks flamed as she felt a small rush of embarrassment.

"Why are you turning red? Don't you know that's one of the reasons I chose you? Your strength and determination, you're willingness to do what it takes for those you love. While you are certainly a beautiful and sensual woman your strength of character far outweighs your physical appearance." He spoke quietly, firmly, and without contempt.

Jane looked at him and felt her cheeks flaming hotter, was she really all of those things? And sensual? Where did that come from?

"Thank you. I've just never thought of myself that way, I suppose. All of those things you said, that just doesn't seem to be me." She fiddled with her glass and looked away.

"But it is you, Jane. You've shown that over the time you've been working at the bar. By now most have given into the temptation for easy money or have turned to drugs to get through their days. You didn't."

"I suppose you're right then. How odd that I've never really thought about it."

You've been too busy for self-reflection I'd imagine." Zare said with blunt honesty.

"This wedding then? It will be big?" She sounded nervous.

"Don't all women want huge weddings with great big giant gowns?" He teased, knowing she wasn't the type for that sort of thing.

"Oh hell no! All those people staring at me, the pressure to surprise, to give the audience what they want? No, not at all. And some of the dresses I've seen? I don't see how women sit down and stand up without a crane to lift them! No, that's too much hassle. A simple civil union, maybe in a garden somewhere, with a few family and close friends is about as much as I can tolerate."

"And the honeymoon?" He asked, a flash sparkling in his gaze, a teasing tone edging into his voice.

"Um. Well." She stuttered to a stop.

"There's that blush again." He teased further.

"Stop!" She protested, grinning at him. "Do we have to do that part? I don't want to leave Charlie for too long. I can't, not really. I wouldn't enjoy myself. I'd be too worried over him."

Zare sobered instantly. He tilted his head as if considering.

"Yes, of course, you're right. When he's better we'll consider it."

Jane could see it was something he hadn't considered and wondered about that oversight. He'd seemed to be so observant about everything else but hadn't considered Charlie being too ill for her to leave him. How could he overlook that?

"May I ask when you'll start taking care of

Charlie's medical bills? I hate to sound business-like but he's not responding to the latest treatment. He needs this new treatment the doctor's spoken about." Jane's words cut off and she looked away. He took her hand across the table and squeezed it reassuringly.

"There's no need to fear discussing anything with me, Jane. I know we've agreed to this wedding for our own reasons but I would like to make it a real marriage someday. Believe in me, trust in me, I will care for both of you as my own. Charlie's new treatment is happening as we speak. I called the hospital earlier and spoke with them about payment and a care plan. Doctor Evans has been instructed to follow your instructions and wishes. He's already been taken care of."

Jane felt tears filling her eyes, her joy and gratitude overwhelming. She almost sobbed in happiness.

"Thank you." That was all she could manage for the moment and held a large linen napkin to her eyes. In that moment she was grateful for the dim candlelight. She could hide in the shadows.

"You're welcome. Now, do you want dessert or do we drive back to see your Charlie?"

"Charlie, please. I'd like to check on him."

Zare paid the bill and soon they sped away in a very expensive sports car that Jane couldn't identify but loved. The tan leather seats seemed to envelope her in luxury and comfort. She looked at the car, at the seemingly simple man across from her and began to wonder. Were the rumors true? Was he a drug dealer? He had money, that was certain, but the kind of money to pay for Charlie's treatment and a car like this? That was more than just dealing drugs. A lot more.

Jane felt a shiver go down her spine and pushed the thoughts away. If it kept Charlie alive she didn't care what Zare was involved in. Not one bit. That might be selfish but she didn't care, Charlie was all that mattered.

Zare took Jane home and went back to his office, a building off the highway, down a long dirt road. For over three hundred years his family owned the property, property that passed from one generation to the next. It was Zare's turn. As the only child of his father he'd inherited the property, the wealth, and the upkeep of the clan.

Over the generations the clan had grown larger, then smaller, fluctuating throughout time. The members of the clan, those that had made the change, lived much longer than the average person, sometimes living up to two or even three centuries before their bodies started to age rapidly before death. Zare was, in fact, 20 years older than the mid-30s that his body displayed, closer to fifty-five than thirty-five. His birth certificate and the deeds to the property reflected his body's age, not his actual age. Having clan members in local government offices helped in that regard.

Keeping a low profile and still running the family business took some effort and Zare was in charge of making sure every member of the clan stayed within the boundaries set up for them by Zare's father, Caleb. Sometimes Zare felt as though he was failing his father and that the clan was endangered by the technological advances the world had produced but he had plans, plans that some disagreed with, but still the best plan for the clan. Time was running out on how long the family business could be maintained, the many fronts they'd used over the generations being phased out by computers and cell phones. There weren't many places left to hide in the world and rather than moving the entire clan to remote part of the world Zare had come up with his current plan. He just had to overcome a few naysayers' objections.

Zare watched as members of the clan counted stacks of plastic wrapped bales and went into the office. Sitting in the chair opposite his desk was one of those naysayers.

"Now, let's discuss how far down in the ground I'll bury you if I hear any more about your machinations and schemes, Joel." Zare sat down, a grim smile on his face as he stared at the black haired man sitting across from him. When the smile disappeared, replaced with a cold malice that was far more threatening, the man began to talk.

Jane changed from the light blue dress she had on and into a pair of yoga pants and a flowing long-sleeved shirt. It was always cold in Charlie's hospital room. She put her long dark hair in a braid, picked out a new e-book and made sure her e-reader's charger was in her handbag. She had a long night ahead of her and she was as prepared as she could be from here.

Jane didn't expect an immediate change in Charlie's health but she felt something she hadn't felt in a very long time crowding out some of the fear and heartache. It took her a moment to realize what it was, a moment to process exactly how she felt. She was halfway to the hospital before it finally crystallized, she'd relaxed. She finally had hope, like the band of terror that had wrapped around her chest all of those weeks ago were finally loosening up a little.

Jane smiled as she pulled into the parking lot of the hospital and walked into the wing of Charlie's ward. She went to his room and her smile, so bright it caught the eye of the nurses, disappeared.

"Nurse? Where's Charlie?" She called out in a panic. He was just here that morning, where was he at now?

"Oh, he's just getting a new line, and his room's been upgraded. He's in 21C now." The nurse said with a smile. "We had a call this afternoon. Congratulations on your engagement by the way. I'm so glad you have something to smile about at this time. Cancer is so hard on the patient but I see so many parents and caretakers in here, they run themselves into the ground for their loved ones and have so little to make them smile. I know it's a tough time but I'm happy for you."

Jane hadn't realized that Zare would work so fast or that he'd put out the word. She hadn't even told Dodie yet! Jane felt her face go pale and knew she had to find her friend. She'd be in Charlie's new room, waiting for Jane. How to explain this? Jane thanked the nurse and went to find the room.

Her steps slowed as she neared the new room, far more private and spacious than the one Charlie had before. It wasn't really that different, they still had to be careful about washing their hands before touching him and other protocols were still in place but the room was brighter with a bigger window and a real bed for whoever was staying with him during the night. That was the biggest change.

Dodie was propped in a recliner watching television when Jane walked in. Dodie looked up with a surprised glance then her eyes went wide.

"I think you have some explaining to do, Cher!" Dodie said as she got up and came to hug her friend. "I don't know how you did it but you just pulled off a miracle!"

7

Jane left the bedroom provided for her on the day of the wedding, Dodie in a suit behind her to carry the train of the gem encrusted white gown Zare had encouraged her to buy on one of their shopping trips. There'd been many in the month since Zare had made his proposal but today was the day. Walking into the backyard, overlooking the Mississippi River of Maison de Fleur, Jane looked back at the huge white plantation home.

Zare proved to not only be rich, but beyond her wildest dreams rich and from one of the oldest families in Louisiana. The family now kept a low profile but were still tightly knit. Jane saw many of Zare's family and friends in the seats but only a few of her family members.

Charlie was improving but couldn't leave the hospital still, and the rest, well Jane just hadn't known or cared enough to invite them.

She and Zare had not been intimate since they'd agreed to this venture but she'd wanted to be with him. Not because of his money but because of the tender care he'd shown and the tempting ways the man had. He'd look at her sometimes and she would wish for a warm bed and their clothes to disappear. Sometimes she even believed that their marriage was a true love-match because he was just so sensitive and caring with her.

She saw him as she came to stand beside him, his dark hair pulled up in its usual knot, his inspiring body hidden beneath a black tuxedo. He made her mouth water with the smoldering look in his eyes and the way his lips parted when he saw her in the halter style dress with the long train. An off-white color, the dress was like something out of her dreams and had cost far more than her car had.

Zare hadn't even batted an eyelid, just looked at her on the pedestal she'd been standing on when she tried it on, and told her this was the one. Jane hadn't wanted to try it on but the sales assistant had encouraged her when he spotted Jane's eyes going back to it over and over. Jane was happy she'd agreed now as she looked up into Zare's eyes and felt a shiver of anticipation. Those eyes promised he'd try to be gentle in taking it off later but he was holding tight to the urge to just rip it off of her now. Even his nostrils flared as he looked down at her.

Jane returned his smoldering stare as she took his hands and the ceremony began. She barely heard it but spoke up when Zare squeezed her hand and she gave the appropriate response. What had started out as a business proposal, a solution to a problem, had turned into far more than she could have hoped for. She wasn't sure but she thought she was falling in love with Zare.

He'd been so kind to Charlie, even coming to visit him and stay with him in the hospital so the boy could get to know him. He'd spent those hours when Charlie was being treated with Jane, talking to her about her past and finding out about her hopes and dreams. He'd arranged a position in the family business, apparently the acquisition and sale of antiquities, and Jane was going to be taking up the position as head of the accounting department. She was looking forward to that.

Zare also had a sense of humor that often set her at ease and she admired the fact that the man with unimaginable wealth spent most of his money on giving back to his community and charities rather than pure pleasure. He even spent a lot of time coaching a local Little League team. Jane heard people laughing and wasn't surprised when she turned her head to see Zare at the center of the laughter.

Jane smiled and thanked people for their well-wishes throughout the night, wondering if there were wolves nearby as darkness fell on the party and she started to hear the howls from the swampland to the left of the property. The plantation home was situated on the banks of the river and surrounded by swampland. Jane had fallen in love with the home immediately and knew Charlie would love exploring the house and the property. Apparently the family members lived out in the swamps in specially built homes high on bracers that protected against flooding. Jane hadn't seen any of them yet but she knew the houses were lovely from the way Zare had described them.

Feeling as though she was watching someone else that evening Jane knew she'd been married but everything had a surreal feel to it. When the males of Zare's family pulled her out to a specially erected dancefloor and started pinning envelopes and money to her dress Jane laughed with happiness. She'd heard about the "money dance" but hadn't seen it really take place. She saw Zare was getting the same treatment as he was passed from one lady to another, much as she was passed from one man to another. She finally ended up in the arms of a man that looked like a much smaller, somehow less handsome version of Zare. This man left her cold, his eyes dead and cruel looking.

"So you're his bride. He picked an outsider. Never mind, you won't be around long anyway." The man sneered down at Jane and dropped his arms before walking away.

Jane stared after the man, wondering what he meant and coming to the realization that not everyone was happy with Zare's choice in his bride. She stood there, her arms hanging at her sides, her hair done up on top of her head in a chic French knot, staring after the man. Then Zare was there, his arms pulling her close.

"What did Brent say to you, love?" He asked as he guided her around the floor.

"Just that I wouldn't be around long. I don't know if that was a threat or if he thought you'd get rid of me. I have no idea but I don't like him." She snuggled closer to her new husband and felt her momentary discomfort leave her as his heat replaced it.

"I'll keep an eye on him. Generally he's harmless but he's been causing problems. His mother is my father's sister. She felt her son should be the Alpha in the clan for some reason. She filled his head with that idea and he's still trying to take it from me. He's never understood that position is given, not taken."

Jane's head began to swim, a combination of the champagne they'd drunk as they cut their cake, the dizzying amount of dancing she'd done, and the entirety of the day. Brent's words hadn't helped but Zare did. Even if his words were just as confusing.

"What's the Alpha mean?" She asked as he pulled her off of the floor and into the house. She waved at Dodie, happily chatting with a female member of Zare's family, as he pulled her into the cool house, out of the heat of the night.

"I'll explain it all soon enough. For now, let's get changed so we can head off to the best part of this night."

"Oh, eager are you?" Jane said with a teasing smile as they went into the room that held their traveling clothes. Jane had chosen a white dress with silver embroidery in the shape of hearts and flowers. It looked surprisingly good on the hanger; she hoped it looked as good on her.

"Believe me, I'd tear your clothes off and pull you down to this bed right now if I could but I want you to myself tonight." He practically growled the words as he pulled off his tie and then his shirt. His clothes weren't as formal, black jeans and a dark grey shirt that showed off his physique replacing the tuxedo and tie.

"Oh my." Jane said as she turned so he could undo her dress.

Somehow they'd both agreed that they were going to head into this as a real relationship, though one that was going slower than most modern relationships today. Jane smiled her thanks back at him before letting the heavy weight of the dress slide away. They were kind of going backwards, they'd already had sex but oh well. The smile stayed in place as she put the other dress on over her bridal lingerie and Zare zipped the dress up with a kiss between her shoulders. This wasn't going to be bad at all.

He took her hand and they went out to their car, the partygoers already assembled to wave goodbye. Jane had no idea where they were going but she didn't care. Charlie was being cared for and it was her wedding night. She was married.

The words sank in and she looked over at Zare driving them to their destination.

"You aren't going to tell me where we're going are you?" She asked.

"Nope. The first part will start in about twenty minutes though." He promised with twinkling eyes.

Zare had driven them to a private airport where a private jet flew them to a private island off the Gulf of Mexico. Zare never did quite say where it was but there were no officials on the island, just a large home with ocean views from all sides, no roads, no power-boats, and lots of solitude. There was no electricity either but a solar water heater was available and a gas stove for cooking.

Jane loved it from the moment she stepped

off of the plane. The house was lit with oil lanterns, and the house stood out amongst palm trees and rock outcroppings. A white palace, Jane wondered how it had withstood hurricanes but forgot her thoughts as Zare picked her up and carried her into the house.

"Welcome to your new life, Mrs. Mallack." He carried Jane into the house and set her down in a gently lit room, large glass doors open to allow the breeze to cool the room. Jane loved how the white curtains blew in the wind.

Zare set her down on a settee and walked to a bottle of champagne sitting in a bucket of ice. Jane had no idea where the ice came from or any of the rest of it but assumed someone had brought it in before they arrived. She took the glass he handed her and smiled up at him in an innocent way that she didn't realize was far more alluring than a sexy pout.

Zare sat down beside her, settling in finally. The day had gone off as he'd hoped, much better than he thought it would. He'd expected some kind of trouble but it hadn't occurred. He and Jane were finally alone, there wasn't anyone else around, and the tempting little minx that had filled his dreams nightly for far too long was finally his. But he needed to make sure she was good with that first.

"Jane, I know we've kind of had this unspoken agreement that we're going to try and make this a real marriage but I have to make sure before I do anything more that this is what you want. I don't want you to feel pressured or as though it's expected of you. We can sit here peacefully for the next two days doing nothing but exploring the island or we can spend it in bed in that other room. It's up to you." He'd looked at her as he spoke but as his words ended he looked down at his now empty champagne glass.

"Zare, you have given me every reason to be grateful to you and I will always feel indebted to you but what we do from here on out has more to do with the person you are than what you can give me. You've been a friend and I needed that. You've given me the world, I can't deny that but you are generous, kind, and sexy as hell. I couldn't say no to you if I tried. And believe me, I tried very hard for a long time. I can't stop how I feel, though. I want this, all of it."

Jane's eyes looked even darker in the lantern light and Zare watched how her lips parted as she watched him. He felt his pulse quickening, his blood pounding through his veins at her merest hint of arousal and hoped he could take his time tonight. He needed her so desperately he was worried he'd rush her.

Jane moved first, climbing into his lap, straddling his hips as her dress pushed up over her hips. Zare's hands went around her hips, touching her, holding her, as she gently lowered herself to him. His face looked up into hers and then their lips met. Jane heard a moan deep in his throat as her hips pressed down into him and the kiss deepened. She pushed down once more and almost giggled when he pulled away to breathe in deeply.

She allowed her hands to stroke down his neck before stroking further down over his hard chest, his flat stomach, before delving deep between them. Jane had to shift to reach the hard ridge of flesh she found in his pants and Zare took the moment to inhale the scent of her neck, his tongue rasping against the sensitive flesh there. Jane gave an involuntary jerk and her hand squeezed at him.

"Neither one of us is going to last like this Jane. Let's go to bed." His ragged breath teased the flesh of her neck and Jane wanted to be naked beneath him on a bed.

"Take me to bed then, Zare." She murmured, pressing into him once more.

She gave a startled "oh" of surprise when he stood and held her to him with ease, carrying her into the bedroom at the top of the stairs. He leaned over the bed, gently dropping her in the middle. Rather than following her down, however, Zare knelt at the side, pulling her satin covered center to his waiting mouth.

"Zare!" She cried out, surprised and pleased, as he pushed her panties aside and breathed on her damp, waiting sex.

"You're beautiful. All of you!" He whispered to her before his lips grazed her bare flesh. His tongue delved between the pink lips of her flesh, splitting her open with his tongue.

Jane felt her body shivering in response to Zare's very intimate touch and sighed. She knew he was a skilled lover but this was beyond anything she'd ever felt before and they'd only just started. His tongue teased her and stroked her, stealing her breath away as he stirred her passions.

Jane's hips started to move, leaving the bed to press into his face, into his mouth, as she suddenly felt his fingers plunge into her tight wetness. His tongue tortured her clit as his fingers delved into her, stretching her for what was to come. She could feel his tongue making tight circles as her body lost control and her cries of pleasure escaped her throat. Jane felt her nipples tightening, abrading against the lace of her bra, teasing her further as Zare's fingers fucked her body, quickly finding her most sensitive spot.

As her breaths came closer together and she started to gasp Zare moved his hands spreading her lower lips to push her clit from its hood. Jane's head thrashed on the bed as Zare sucked at the sensitive button, the sensations almost more than she could bare but she didn't want it to stop either. She'd never felt anything so primitive, so sexually satisfying, as Zare's lips sucking at her clit!

Jane's body tensed and she stopped breathing for a moment as her body contracted from head to toe. When the wave finally broke over her she gave a harsh cry of pleasure, far more guttural than anything she thought she could ever make and she lost herself to unstoppable pulses shooting through her.

Zare watched her writhing beneath him and had to stop himself from getting up and plunging his hard flesh into her soft, giving flesh. His cock hardened even more, watching Jane as she came apart above him. He'd never felt anything so stirring as watching his wife coming. He felt a tingle in his chest as he realized she was indeed his wife, and sucked hard once more to let her keep riding the waves.

Zare eased off as the pleasure making her stomach muscles contract started to slow, letting her ease down to earth once more. Wiping his mouth of her juices Zare sat back on his heels and admired his wife.

"Think you can spend your life getting that princess?" He asked as he got up and undressed himself. He watched her, a broad smile on her face as she slowly opened her eyes.

"I didn't think that was really possible. But yes, you can do that any time you want to." Jane replied slowly, her eyes closing once more as she floated in somewhere between bliss and reality.

"Oh, I plan to after seeing the response it got. For now, I'd like to see the rest of you. Your soft skin, your body, has haunted my dreams. I need to see you bared for my eyes only, princess. I can't wait anymore." Zare said, pulling her up so he could part the zipper at her back and pull her dress from her body.

Jane felt the dress slipping away and hoped the lingerie she'd picked out was pleasing. She had on a white lace bra that cupped her large round breasts in their depths. A waist corset cinched her waist in white satin and below that rested a pair of rather scandalous white lace panties. White stockings clung to her thighs and Jane felt beautiful as Zare let his eyes caress her body greedily.

His hands soon followed, his lips close behind. Zare leaned over the bed, his right knee propping his body up as he explored his new wife's body. His lips grazed down her neck before swooping down to her left breast. Her nipple pushed through the lace and Zare could see her nipples were a dusky rose in the lantern light.

Pushing the delicate material away Zare tasted Jane's nipple tentatively, first giving it a long lave with his tongue before sucking the crinkled flesh between his lips. Jane's chest pushed into his mouth as her hips pushed down into the bed, pressing her clitoris between her thighs.

"Oh, don't stop." Jane urged, loving the sensations Zare created within her. He increased her pleasure by sliding his other leg up on the bed and pressing it between her thighs, giving her something to clamp down on.

He then took her other nipple between his fingers as he bit down gently on her nipple. Rather than creating pain the bite sent a wave of desire burning through Jane's insides. Jane all but purred when she felt Zare move and his hard flesh pressed into the slick heat he'd created with his attentions.

Jane's yelp of pleasure, a sweet sound that pierced straight into Zare's skull and down to his cock finally broke him. He could feel her slickness against his thigh and he needed to be inside of her. He could remember how tight she was, how oh so hot and slick she felt wrapped around his dick in that instant and he just couldn't stop himself.

Nudging her thighs apart Zare moved into place, his fingers finding her opening as he guided his rigid flesh into her. His heat sought hers and he groaned in pleasure as he sank into her intoxicating body. Jane wasn't thin, she had cushion that delighted him, breasts that amazed him, and a wet pussy that had him gritting his teeth against the urge to just fuck her mindlessly until he came.

Zare felt his wolf wanting to take control and clamped down on it, clinching his jaw tightly. He stilled his hips, not letting them press deeper yet. He waited for Jane's signal and when she moved, pressing up into him, he knew he could start the slide that would take him deeper into this beautiful woman.

Zare felt his cock sliding into Jane's grasping body and shivered.

"You feel so fucking good, Jane." He gasped, grasping at her hips, his fingers digging into her soft flesh.

Jane felt her muscles contract deep inside at his words and felt his fingers tighten on her hips. Knowing he was enjoying her body was tantalizing, it gave her a sense of power, and she moved faster, urging him to go deeper, harder, with her body.

Zare responded, leaning over, pressing his hands to each side of her head as he thrust into her, his face a mask of concentration as he fucked into her, taking all Jane offered as she spread her thighs wider, pressing up into him.

Jane felt his slick shoulder muscles, his body starting to perspire as he made love to her in the dimly lit room. Her own body was growing damp in the heat of their passion, and they moved together slickly. She yelped in surprise when he moved away from her, pulling out of her body to flip her over. When she was on her hands and knees, her face pressed into a pillow Zare entered her once more with one hard thrust and made her scream in pleasure.

His hands buried in her hair as his wolf finally took some of his control, an urge to bite gently into the back of her neck almost too much to hold back. He had to satisfy himself with his hands in her hair, pressing her down into the covers as he took her more than willing body. Over and over Zare thrust into his woman, claiming her, as his wolf claimed her as well.

He could smell her excitement, her thrill at being taken in this way. The smell oozed from her skin and from the juices flowing from her pussy. She wanted him, she needed him, and Zare gave himself gladly, his body finally letting go as he heard her crying out his name as her pussy began to convulse around him, milking his cock into coming with her as she fell over the edge once more.

Their souls mated as their bodies melted, and Jane felt as though Zare was in her body with her as they exploded together. Zare pulsed into her quivering body, emptying himself inside her with sharp thrusts of his hips. He felt himself sliding into her with his seed, his soul touching hers and becoming entangled for a moment, no longer than a breath but it felt like an eternity, before he slipped back into his own body.

"What was that?" Jane asked a few moments later. He'd come up beside of her, pulling a silky cotton sheet over their bodies as he took her in his arms.

With Jane on his chest Zare suddenly felt what it was like to love a woman, to have a mate for life. Yes, his decision had been right, that first time hadn't just been a fluke, and they were mated forever now.

"I don't know but it rocked my world." Zare told her, not sure of how to explain it without giving away secrets he needed to hide for a while longer, until he was sure she could handle the truth.

"Yeah, earth shattering, world rocking. Whatever it was, it was fantastic."

Zare breathed a contented sigh and pulled her more tightly to his chest. She was his wife and somehow she'd just changed his whole world. She was his world now and that changed things. Maybe for the better.

8

Jane pulled herself from her memories of her honeymoon of midnight strolls along the beach before making love in the ocean, to her present reality of smiling at people she still wasn't sure of. She'd been Zare's wife for over a month now and the Sunday family dinners still felt awkward for her.

She'd been watching a group of males ranging in age from 18 to 64 for the last hour. They kept breaking apart and coming back together. They would shift between glaring at Zare's back and turning away when he turned in their direction. All cousins of Zare's, she couldn't ask them to leave but she didn't have to stand around watching them glaring at her husband when his back was turned.

A month of marriage produced a deep abiding love within Jane for Zare. The man was everything she'd expected him to be and more. He might not be her childhood dream of what a man should be but she loved him deeply regardless. He was exactly what she'd needed, not a fantasy. There was more to the family and the family business than she was being told but she wasn't too concerned. After all, Zare couldn't be doing anything wrong.

They still made the occasional jaunt out to the bar but for the most part Zare stayed home with her at the end of the day. He'd go out to play in his pool league games, to operate his business, and to get things done but for the most part he stayed near Jane, even moving a lot of his work to the office in the house.

But that look of malice from his cousins, what did that mean? The clan was something Zare often spoke of, the good of the clan, the future of the clan. These men, and a previous mention of the Alpha, made Jane wonder. She kept telling herself Zare couldn't be involved in anything bad but why else would those men be looking at him like that. Did it mean they resented what he was doing or did it mean they wanted part of what he had?

Jane brushed off her concerns as Zare's aunt, Star, came up to show Jane a new book she'd ordered. Jane gave the expected responses but kept Zare in her sights. She was worried about him. Later she lost sight of Zare and saw the group of men talking together as they moved out to a barn a little further back from the house.

The land here had been reclaimed from the swamp but it still took a lot of work to keep the swamp from claiming it back. Jane watched the men and followed, noticing that there were quite a few people coming in and out of the barn, some hanging out around the outside. She went to the back of the barn, the encroaching night and a few cypress trees hiding her movements.

She found a window and looked into the barn. What she saw made her nearly fall off of the barrel she was perched on. Inside there was a boxing ring, tables and chairs, and a crowd of people. That explained all of the boats parked behind the house. She'd wondered where all of those people were.

Jane smothered a gasp behind her hand as

she spotted two men going into the ring. There was no referee and the two men started pounding at each other as soon as they walked into the ring. Both were in their late 40s and overweight, balding, and looked like the last place they belonged was in a boxing ring.

Blood was soon pouring from one of the men and as he fell to the floor of the ring the other man leaped onto his chest a knife appearing from somewhere. He pushed the blade deep into the man's skin but he didn't stab him. Instead he looked up and following his line of sight. Jane felt her world start to collapse again. Zare was standing there shaking his head.

The victor growled and punched the fallen man in the face once more before he stomped off. Jane wobbled on the barrel but grabbed at the window sill. No wonder Zare had told her it was too dangerous in the barn for her! Jane felt tears pricking her eyes as she saw women taking money from men and leading them off to dark corners of the barn while others handed over pills.

Jane didn't recognize any of the prostitutes or the people buying pills but the room was swarming with Zare's people, members of the bike gang, and other members of the clan. What the hell was going on? Is this how Zare made his money? Jane saw Charlie's face flash before her eyes and knew, in that moment, that it didn't matter.

She loved Charlie, he was the reason she'd married Zare. She hadn't married him to feel safe, loved, or secure, she'd married him for the life-saving treatment that had worked so well Charlie was now at home with her and Zare, his own room outfitted to take care of his medical leave, a private doctor and nurse visiting him daily.

And if she was completely honest with herself, she loved Zare. She didn't know how but she'd learn to live with knowing that the man she loved wasn't exactly a saint. So long as it didn't threaten Charlie or her, she'd look past it. Jane saw Zare coming out of the back door of the barn and tried to hop down from the barrel to disappear but stumbled and fell instead.

"What are you doing out here princess? Come on, I need a shower and you beneath me." He grinned at her as he helped her up and pulled her close.

Jane stiffened for a moment but made herself

relax. Nothing had changed, she told herself, not really. She'd just had a dose of reality; she had to live with that now. She melted into him, praying his touch would make it all go away. That man's life had depended on a decision Zare made. Jane shivered but when Zare's lips met hers she pushed the memory away and gave herself up to her husband.

Life went on as normal but Jane continued to keep an eye on The Faction as she'd come to think of the group of men. Something was going on and it was stressing her. Luckily Charlie seemed to be improving and that eased some of her stress but every bit of her that gained relief seemed to be taken up by this group of men. What were they up to, what were they planning?

Now that Jane knew what happened out in the barn she kind of suspected what was going on. Nothing showed up through the business section so she couldn't prove it through the accounting but that wasn't just a coincidence out in the barn. And it wasn't something that was new. That man had looked at Zare as though this was a regular occurrence, not a once in a lifetime thing.

Jane felt the nagging of the questions, the

worry, and finally decided a few weeks later to confront Zare about it. She'd promised herself she wouldn't but she was worried this might somehow impact Charlie. She felt some concern that questioning Zare about his family's business might result in a negative reaction but she felt she was owed an explanation. He'd kept hinting at things, making comments offhand only to backtrack when he realized what he'd said.

Jane put her worry to rest as she found him and he took her in his arms. There with the door to his office closed Jane realized that they'd become partners, though unequal at the moment. Zare would listen to her concerns and address them. He wouldn't throw Charlie and her out just because she asked some questions.

Zare leaned down to kiss her and Jane moved away, not wanting to be distracted. She left his arms and sat on the black leather couch at one of the office, patting the spot beside her. She saw him looking at her, observing the way her face was set and she saw realization dawning.

"Ah. It's that time finally. Right then, my love." Zare came to sit beside her and took her hand. "I guess you saw more than I thought that night I found you behind the barn?"

Jane shook her head positively, looking at him mutely for the moment.

"You need answers. Have we got some time or will Charlie need you soon?" He asked, pushing her dark hair behind her ear.

"No, his nurse is there for now. I have a few hours." She spoke, her voice wobbly. She cleared her throat and looked up at him bravely. "What's going on? I want to know all of it."

"I have to start at the beginning. Three hundred years ago my grandfather was bitten by a wild animal, a wolf as it turns out. He was the leading farmer around here growing whatever would earn him the most profit. His land was fertile and he knew what to grow here. He became rich beyond his dreams but he also became cursed. That bite made him...change." Zare looked away for a moment.

"He kept to himself for a long time, his sons and their wives were pushed away, out of the house, and into houses he had built around the property. For many months he hid away in this office, keeping everyone at bay. Until finally, one winter night, a night with a full moon, a wild animal attacked many of his family members, killing several small children."

Jane gasped at several points in the story but clung to Zare. She knew where this was heading. She'd heard rumors about these "animals" for years now but hadn't put much belief in them. They were just stories to scare children away from the swamp, that was all. Right?

"At the next full moon the family members all turned, more people were bitten, and when it was all done, when people emerged from their homes and tried to make it through the aftermath, they finally discovered what they were from Grandfather. He'd been turned into a shifter, a werewolf, whatever you want to call us. We call ourselves shifters."

Zare looked up at her, pulling his head from where he'd bowed it as he spoke to her. Jane could see his black eyes changing, a yellow she'd never seen in a human's eyes flashing and sparking in their depths. Fear crept into her heart and her pulse raced as the eyes continued to change, the yellow pushing back the darkness of the black.

Zare growled for a moment and Jane sat back, her pulse jumping. Then the black pushed the yellow away and his eyes went back to normal. There was definitely more to Zare than she'd ever dreamed possible.

"So you're, you..." Her words trailed off, her brain not able to form the words she sought to speak.

"A shifter, yes. We've kept this secret, or tried to, for generations now. But now it's time to tell the world. Far too many of our number have disappeared into research facilities, have been killed, and honestly, it's just becoming harder to hide who and what we are. We need protection from the outside world, to do that we have to reveal ourselves." Zare's face had tensed when she'd moved away in fear but he was relaxing now.

Jane knew part of the reason he was relaxing was because she was. She couldn't believe she was still sitting there but she loved her brother and she loved this man. She had also seen those eyes of his. Those weren't normal eyes. There was far more there than she knew about or could understand. She thought about asking him to prove he could shift into a wolf but part of her didn't want to see that. Not yet anyway.

"Is that why The Faction keeps following you

around? They don't want the secret out?" Jane asked, taking his hand in hers.

"The Faction? Oh, you mean my cousins? Yes, they are a problem and something we have to keep an eye on. They don't realize I know but their plan is to turn as many humans as they can and kill the rest. They think they can be kings of a new planet, a new lifeform for the earth. They don't realize the chaos they could cause instead. It will be chaotic enough to reveal ourselves, there's a lot of fear in this world today, but we don't need what those assholes have in mind."

Jane gave a rueful smile and stayed quiet, letting him speak.

"I need you to keep all of this to yourself right now, Jane. I wouldn't blame you if you ran screaming from here but I'd never harm you. I can't promise the rest of the clan won't though." Zare looked at her with worry and fear.

"Is that what your cousin meant on our wedding day? He planned on getting rid of me?" Jane felt fear turn her blood cold.

"Perhaps. It's hard to tell with Brent. He's a loose cannon I can't do anything about yet, now without permission of the whole clan. We have to deal with him for now, unfortunately."

"Alright. Well, I'm not going anywhere, and I'm certainly not going to be running my mouth about it. Thank you for telling me, Zare." He looked surprised when she stood up and walked to his office door. She was surprised herself but she needed time to think.

"I'm certain of my decision darling, and I give you my vow of silence on the matter. But I need to see Charlie, I need to think. Give me a few hours? I just need to process this." She gave him a pleading smile and he nodded his head, his concern apparent. "I'll be in Charlie's room, darling. I'll see you later."

Jane slipped out of the door and for a moment considered running for Charlie's room and dragging him out of this place. She had to stop and steady herself halfway to his room. What the hell had she gotten them into?

Jane headed in the direction of Charlie's room, lost in her thoughts. Zare was some kind of shapeshifter? He actually *turned into a wolf*? Her natural instinct was to scoff and call the men in white coats but those eyes of his had told her all she needed to know. Human eyes couldn't change color at will.

She was in a quiet wing of the three story

sprawling mansion when she heard something behind her. She looked but didn't see anything. When she turned back around she saw the shape of a man dressed in black and what looked like a white cloth coming straight for her face. Jane struggled, kicking and punching at the two assailants trying to hold her still.

Jane knew there must be something on the cloth but couldn't stop the urge to scream, inhaling a large dose of whatever was on the cloth as she inhaled to give the scream life. Her struggles eased as the drug worked into her system, the edges of the world going dark before fading to black. As Jane slumped into the arms of the man behind her they pulled her to another part of the house before carting her outside to a waiting car.

9

"She's coming around!"

Jane heard the words and felt them like an assault on her brain as she woke up with the worst headache she'd ever had. She moaned, confused as to why she hurt so bad and where she was. Cracking her eyelids open she saw the blurry shape of four men standing over her in a dark room. This wasn't a room in her home, though, the walls were rough-hewn wood and there was no window. Where was she?

"What's going on? Where am I?" Jane tried to sit up but the impact of a fist against her right cheek made her reel back, the shock of feeling such a powerful impact and being struck outweighing the pain for a moment. She struggled to move away from the fist and got a punch in the kidneys for her trouble.

"Stay still, stop moving, and just sit there, bitch. Do not move!" The male voice sounded familiar but Jane was too stunned to place the voice.

She moved her hand slightly, reaching up to touch the area just below her eye and before she could even reach the swelling skin furious fists were hitting her from all sides. Jane curled into a ball, screaming at her assailant to stop as her face took the brunt of the beating. As she moved to protect her face his fists cracked against her wrist and she felt the bones snap before his fist met her jaw once more. Pain exploded in her head and the screams stopped as shock took over. She was totally terrified and unable to escape the pounding fists that bruised her flesh, tore her skin, and left her a mewling mess on a rudimentary bed. The beating only took minutes but Jane experienced it as a lifetime of terror and pain.

"I said stay still, bitch. Do as you're told and you won't get hurt!" The angry voice held some note that made Jane even more afraid. It sounded like excitement!

She shuddered on the bed, her body and mind in shock, unable to think beyond a keen need for Zare. Even that was soon overwhelmed by the pain of her battered body and Jane passed out, certain her arm was broken, that her jaw might be too, and that she was bleeding from several places where his fists and rings had cut her flesh.

Zare walked through the house, looking for his wife. Fear had started to worm its way into his heart as he searched the rooms three hours after their talk. Jane hadn't come to him; she hadn't been seen by anyone. Had his revelation scared her into running? Zare headed for Charlie's room, knowing Jane would never leave him behind if she'd been that afraid.

He quietly opened the door to Charlie's room and felt a moment of relief to see the boy asleep in his bed. Charlie had wormed his way into Zare's heart with his courage and determination to beat cancer so that his sister didn't have to be alone. He'd eyed Zare up quite a few times, as though deciding whether he'd allow the man into Jane's life or not, but then he'd made his decision. Since then Charlie had done his best to be a trooper for his sister and his brother-in-law. Zare was proud of the child and admired his determination. He was glad to see that the child was still there but it also increased his worry. Where was Jane?

Zare closed the door and quickly reached for his madly vibrating phone as it buzzed away in the pocket of his black jeans. Striding quietly out of the hall and down to another part of the house Zare answered with a terse hello.

"We have your bitch Zare. Abdicate your Alpha throne to Brent or she dies. We might have a little fun with her first, if we can get past how ugly her face is now. You have one day to make it happen. That's it. Set it in motion or she's going to disappear from the face of the earth. And guess who always gets that blame for missing spouses? So either way, you lose dickhead but we'd rather not have to kill her so make the right choice."

Zare started to speak, to demand answers, but the phone went dead and he was left standing in an empty hallway. Zare stood breathing heavily, his anger and fear rising. He knew who had Jane and exactly where they were. Dialing a number in his phone he made the first of many calls to assemble his boys. He was going to get his wife back.

Jane stirred in the darkness, all of the lights now out in the room she was being held in, and tried not to cry out as her very swollen arm, her bruised ribs, and her face protested even the slightest of movements. She'd learned her lesson, stay still and stay quiet. That was hard to do with all of her aches and pains but then her bladder kicked in and started to raise a fuss. She was terrified of getting hit or kicked again so she just kept still, hoping that she wasn't breathing too hard.

She cracked an eyelid, looking around once more, but the room was pitch black and she couldn't see anything. She calmed her breathing, hoping it would help her hear better but she heard nothing. She couldn't smell anything but the cloth in the room and the wood, her own fear maybe, but nothing more, nothing that would tell her where she was.

Sensing she was alone for now she tried to move but as soon as she put any kind of pressure on her right arm it exploded with pain and she fell back, holding back a scream with her left hand. She'd also felt her ribs and face protesting and knew she wasn't going to go far, not when the nausea from the pain hit her in waves.

Still in shock Jane let her head fall to the pillow once more and let the darkness take her. She was terrified of what might come next and wanted only to sleep, to stay unaware of just how much trouble she was in.

Sleep wouldn't come though and she had to hide a scream of fear when a man opened a door and walked into the room. She knew it was a man by the low chuckle he gave when he walked in.

"Not so high and mighty now, are we missy? You're just trash, refuse. Your man ain't even called to save you yet. I guess he knows he's fucked either way so he's left you to me."

Jane tensed; it was the same man from earlier. The same voice of the man who had threatened her at the wedding. Zare had called him Brent. She shrieked involuntarily when he pulled at her legs, wrenching at the buttons of her jeans. Oh no, not this, she'd take another beating over this.

"Do that again bitch and I'll beat your head in. Don't push me." He grabbed her aching jaw, making her cry out in pain, before he went back to her pants. Jane tried to kick him, tried to move away from him desperately but he wouldn't let her go far. He punched her in the stomach and Jane doubled up as her air supply suddenly disappeared.

"Stay still or I'll just knife you and get it over with."

Jane stilled, hoping her brain would retreat, praying for the blackness she knew could come. She tried not to beg him to stop but her lips moved, even as her voice disappeared. Brent was sliding her pants off of her legs, making her want to vomit as his fingers trailed up her smooth skin. Please no, her lips mouthed, please no.

Just as the man pushed himself between her thighs, fumbling at his pants, someone came through the door, flipped on a light switch, and Brent turned, yelling his displeasure at the person. Jane heard a loud noise and then Brent slumped against her body, something warm and wet spreading across her chest where his head rested.

Jane fought back the urge to scream but lost and pushed with her legs, looking down to see a hole going straight through the middle of Brent's head.

"Stop screaming. Your man will be here soon enough and I don't need your shrieks distracting me. Jay, get in here and get rid of this mess. Feed him to the gators!" The man turned and left the room as Jane hid her face in a pillow. Would this nightmare never end?

ZARE LISTENED TO SETH AND GLEN DISCUSSING how best to enter the house in the swamp without being detected. He got tired of waiting, made sure his gun was loaded once more, and went up the steps from the boat ramp at the bottom of the house built directly over the swamp. He moved quietly, noting that his men followed, before he came to a door and pushed it open. He started firing his gun as soon as he opened the door.

Walking into the room a few moments later

he saw several men on the ground, injured to varying degrees, but paid them no attention. Going through the rooms he finally found Jane in one of them. He roared in rage when he saw her condition and gathered her into his arms. Jane came back to reality as she felt Zare near and clung to him with her uninjured arm.

Before they left Zare paused and told Jane to turn her head. Jane tensed, wondering, knowing what was coming. She knew the men deserved it but as Zare shot each man, killing them, Jane's denial finally snapped. Charlie was in danger from this, she was too, but this was far too much for her to handle and to expose Charlie to.

Zare called a doctor to come and tend to her wounds once she was bathed and tucked into bed but Jane refused the medicine. Zare refused to leave her side for the rest of the night, holding her as she shivered in the darkness, but he had to go to work the next morning.

Acting fast Jane found the safe where Zare hid some money, entered the code, and took out $50,000 in cash. It would be hard to explain if she was caught with it but she knew she needed it. She threw some clothes in a bag, then went to Charlie's room. He was stronger now but still weak. She gathered some things for him and had the nurse help her carry her brother out to one of the cars in the garage. Then, with her splinted arm, she started to drive. She drove for two days straight, driving until she could barely see anymore.

She threw her phone away in Texas, ditched her tablet in Oklahoma, and finally located the GPS tracking device on the car in Kansas. She pulled that off and carried on driving. When she saw an empty house on a back country road in Montana she went to a payphone to call the number listed. She then found a second hand shop in the nearest town and bought every bit of furniture they had in the place. She paid them two weeks wages to deliver it that day.

The one thing she did not buy was a new cellphone or anything else that Zare could use to track her. She bought Charlie a game console and a TV but no computers, no phones, no way to communicate. Not right now, she couldn't handle it right now. Tomorrow, once she'd slept, she'd buy a phone in case of emergencies, but she cooked some dinner, gave Charlie his meds, and made up their beds.

Her last thought after falling into bed was

how she was going to provide Charlie with what he needed. He had a month's supply of his pills but after that he'd be out and she knew she'd have to provide his medical charts to get the medicine. She decided that was another worry for tomorrow just before she fell asleep, exhaustion finally taking over.

She slept for twelve hours and Charlie finally woke her up only because he'd run out of stuff to make sandwiches with.

"I don't want to wake you up, sis, I know you're hurt so bad and scared but I'm hungry. I don't know how to cook anything." Charlie looked ashamed for a moment and Jane's heart broke as she came awake and rubbed at her eyes.

"It's okay Charlie, I'm hungry too. Let me use the bathroom and I'll fix us some food, alright?" She hugged him gently, knowing he was just as fragile as she was, and fumbled her way through using the bathroom and cleaning her face. She'd tried to shield Charlie from what had happened to her, and why she'd left, but she couldn't hide her face from him. Swollen and turning a variety of colors, she'd had some strange looks, but most had turned to sympathy when she'd asked about the house and buying furniture and linens for a house.

Jane guessed they all assumed she was running from an abusive spouse. Zare had been anything but abusive but he'd lived a life of violence. She couldn't expose Charlie to that. Besides, as the day approached when Zare and the clan intended to expose their kind to the world, she knew she and Charlie would be in even more danger. Only a few more days to go, then she and Charlie might be safe but for now she knew she had to hide them from the world. She had to keep them safe. Zare couldn't do that.

A MONTH HAD GONE BY, A MONTH OF HEALING, quiet, and peace for both Charlie and Jane. She'd had to break her silence to get his medical records sent to the small town doctor but so far things had remained quiet. They were in a restaurant in town now, watching Zare being interviewed by a talk show host.

Jane cradled her stomach, a move that would soon become a habit as her pregnancy progressed. She and Zare were going to be parents but he didn't know that. She still didn't know how far along she was but the doctor had told her today they could soon deduce that with an ultrasound.

Jane watched the television screen in the restaurant, reading the closed captioning that ran along the bottom. Zare had finally accomplished his dream, the world knew about the clan in Louisiana now. Apparently Louisiana was the wolf-shifter capital of the world and though many hadn't been happy to be exposed, a great deal more agreed with Zare's thinking. Protection from the machinations of those that plotted evil and harm was important.

For generations the shifters had hidden from the world, to protect the people of the world and the shifter community, but now they were being used as military weapons. Hopefully that would stop now, at least the involuntary use, if someone wanted to volunteer for that so be it. Now they had a choice.

Jane was proud of Zare but she knew there were still secrets there. Secrets that she could not deal with. She missed her husband, she missed his easy smile, the way he'd make her laugh, the way he rocked her world in bed, but Charlie, and now their baby, were too important to her to abandon for her own selfish needs.

Jane saw that Charlie was finished with his dinner and signaled to the waitress to bring their bill. Time to get home and back to the safety of their quiet world. Jane felt exposed and wanted the quiet solitude of the ranch-style house she and Charlie now lived in. She hugged the boy close as they walked out of the restaurant, arguing over which brownie mix they were going to bake tonight. This was what was most important to her.

10

Zare had known all along where Jane was, he just knew she needed time to process what had happened to her and what she'd seen. Part of him knew she could be so terrified she'd run forever, but he told himself she just needed time. The first time Charlie had logged into his game console's web service he'd known where they were. He gave her the space she so obviously needed.

He'd kept tabs on her through a wolf-shifter he'd sent up to the town she was living in, a young, gentle woman named Mona. Mona didn't approach Jane or Charlie, she just kept tabs on them and who else might be in the small town. That was one good thing about the place Jane chose, outsiders stuck out like sore thumbs.

"So, we have reports that they're looking for Jane again?" Zare asked the woman sitting across from him. Beautiful and smart, Ruby had been seeing a lot of Jane's friend Dodie, which was good because it kept her occupied and prevented questions about Jane's whereabouts, but could be problematic as Ruby didn't like keeping things from her loved ones.

"Yes, some of the women from over around Houma are hearing their men discussing it. They are saying if they can't shut you up they'll hurt you. Unfortunately, that's made Jane a target. Again." Ruby looked at Zare pointedly, her displeasure noticeable.

"If I'd known this was going to happen I'd have done something more to prevent it. I didn't know." The entire clan had looked at Zare with anger when news of Jane's abduction and assault was spread amongst them. The family knew why Zare had killed the men that abducted her, the clan needed to be shown he could do it and would. They didn't understand why he'd allowed any of it to happen. "I hoped it wouldn't come to that. I know better now."

"Good. When are we going to retrieve her?"

Ruby asked, her foot tapping against the oak floor in anticipation.

"I, and I alone, will be going for her tonight. Get the jet ready." Zare knew he could give directions to most of his lieutenants and they'd follow his command without question. Ruby was just the same as her male counterparts.

The jet flew through the dark night, and his body tensed as he neared the airport. He'd have to drive the rest of the way but it wouldn't take long. Then he'd see the woman he'd realized he loved when he pulled her from that cabin in the swamp. Seeing her broken and beaten hadn't just caused him to lash out to prove to his clan he was strong, it had caused him to lash out in anger and despair at what those bastards had done to her. He'd let her go to protect her, to give her what she seemed to want.

Now he had to bring her back, to keep her safe from his world. Zare felt his heart squeeze as he realized he'd caused her this grief. He told himself that what he'd done had been for the best though. Charlie would not have survived without him. They'd both needed what he could offer and he'd given it to them.

Zare followed the guidance of the GPS until

he found a long dirt driveway and followed it up to the unlit house. He saw a flicker in the windows and realized there was a television on in the house at least. He knew she must have seen the lights from his car as he pulled up but she didn't come to a window or the door. Maybe she was asleep on the couch?

He smiled at how sweet the thought was and got out of the car. His nerves made him jumpy but he could appreciate the beauty of the quiet house, almost hidden in the pine trees around it. It was peaceful and homey, just what she'd like.

He took a deep breath and walked up on her porch. He knocked when he couldn't spot a doorbell and waited, his hands clenched in front of him as he waited. Would she order him off the property? Scream and throw the door shut?

He didn't have to wait long before he heard her footsteps moving through the house and a chain and lock being removed. At least she was smart enough to keep the doors locked he thought just before the door opened and she gasped.

Jane kind of suspected who was knocking at her door but told her pulse to slow down. Maybe it was the owner of the rental property, or that nice lady that worked at the restaurant. Sometimes she brought pies around for Charlie. But her gut told her it was too late for any of them to be coming round, and her pulse told her it was Zare. Her body knew, even if her mind refused to accept it.

She saw his eyes widen as she opened the door, taking in her lightened hair, now a soft brown, and the change in clothing style. Jane was normally a cheap PJs when at home kind of girl, or a casual but business-like attire when going out. She'd worn cheap clothes at the bar but now she wore silk pajamas and her hair was different. His eyes widened as his gaze fell to her stomach and he looked up at her.

"You're pregnant?" He whispered as if awestruck.

Her hand went to her stomach and she gasped. "How did you know?"

"We're connected now, and I'll always be able to sense where my children are, the same as you'll be able to. May I come in?" He asked, needing to sit down. He was going to be a father.

She hesitated, afraid of the baggage Zare brought with him but there was something different in his eyes, something soft. Perhaps it was only the child that softened his gaze but when his eyes sent her a pleading glance she gave in. Opening the door she stepped back and held her arm out.

"Would you like something to drink?" She asked politely, wanting to giggle at how very perfunctory she sounded. This was her husband and she was treating him like a guest.

"Coffee if you have it. It's been a long day." He said as he took a seat on a stool in the kitchen. He was sitting at the island, watching her make coffee in the kitchen of the old farmhouse.

"I suppose it was if you came here all the way from Louisiana after that interview. What brings you out here?" She stamped down on her need to have him say he wanted her to come home. She hadn't run all this way just to go all wimpy on herself now. She'd run for a reason.

"I need you to hide. I know that's why you're here but I found you the moment you stopped and settled down. Anybody else that's looking can do that too."

"How?" She demanded to know. She could

have sworn there was no way to find her. Even the electric was in the property owner's name!

"Charlie's game console account. It was that simple." Granted not everyone would think to look for her that way but it showed how it was next to impossible to hide in today's world.

"Wow. I didn't even think of that. So we're in danger again? Did you bring it with you this time as well?" She knew the words stung but she couldn't stop herself from saying them to him. She was glad Charlie was in bed now and wasn't here to see Zare. He loved Zare and had asked when they were going home every day since they'd left.

Jane tried to make the boy understand it was just too dangerous but he knew Jane loved Zare, he loved Zare, and Zare loved them. Isn't that all that mattered? Jane hadn't been able to answer that and had changed the subject.

"I hope I haven't brought it with me this time." Zare said, bringing her back to the present. And I know where to hide you this time."

"And where's that? Have you got us seats on the International Space Station?" Jane's raised eyebrow was a challenge from across the island.

"Not quite, no. Maison de Fleur has a hidden apartment. Only my father and grandfather knew about it, a few servants a long time ago. I plan to take you there." Zare looked away from her when she scoffed in disbelief.

"To the very house I was abducted from? I don't think so buddy. Not going to happen!" She turned to pour him a cup of coffee, adding the cream he'd got her addicted to in their time together.

"No, hear me out. It's like a kid's dream palace in there. Hidden walls, hidden doors, you can't find it without going through my bedroom and only then if you know how to get the door to open. There are no windows but there are two bedrooms, a bathroom, a kitchen, and a living room. I've updated it over the years so it's comfortable but it's where I go when I need to get away from the family for a while. None of them know about it, I swear Jane."

"I'll think about it. How long have I got?" She breathed through her mouth forcefully, letting him know she wasn't happy.

"Until mid-afternoon tomorrow. I want to take you both in when it's dark out. Nobody knows where I am at the moment except my most trusted people. The rest think I'm in New York doing an interview."

"Alright. Well. You can sleep on the couch for the night. I'm going to bed." She brushed by suddenly needing to get away from him so she could think without him nearby to distract her.

"Please Jane. Come with me." His eyes pleaded with her but she pushed away.

"I'll let you know in the morning."

She went into her room and turned off the light, knowing a pillow and a blanket were on the couch that he could use. Jane heard him settling in on the couch and wondered if he was undressing. For an instant a memory of Zare's naked body filled her mind and she squirmed in the bed, knowing it was going to be a long night with him so close.

He looked tired, and thinner. She didn't like that. She knew he was having a rough time and that must be the reason behind it. Revealing such a huge secret to the world couldn't be easy on a man. Sighing she rolled over, punching her pillows.

Perhaps she should invite him into her bed? It was king size, there was plenty of room, even for him. That's when she realized he hadn't mentioned the money she'd taken. Maybe he just didn't care about the money? Maybe he knew she'd needed something to keep them safe and wasn't going to say anything about it. Even with the purchases she'd made most of it was still hidden in the lining of her suitcase in the closet.

Jane let her mind wander, thinking about nonsense to distract herself. Her body craved her husband, craved his touch, and she'd left the room rather than give in to that need. Now she couldn't stand knowing he was so close but not touching her. After so many weeks apart to see him now was torture. She'd kidded herself into believing she hadn't missed him but she had. And now she could hear him clearing his throat in the other room.

Maybe he'd slip into bed with her when she fell asleep. Slide his hands into her silky pants, between her thighs, and tease her into exploding in his arms? Or maybe she'd go to him, slip under the cover and straddle him. Jane had to bite back a moan as she imagined riding him until he inhaled sharply and pumped his pleasure into her?

"Fuck!" The word slipped quietly from Jane's

lips, a word she rarely said but often thought. She was frustrated and it was taking a toll.

This wasn't helping she decided as she rolled in the bed again, spreading her legs so her thighs wouldn't press into her center. How was she going to get to sleep now? Go in there and let him take the ache away or do it herself?

She was just about to throw her covers off when she heard gentle snores coming from the living room through the bedroom door. That settled that question then. She listened to his snores, glad that he was sleeping at least. What was she going to do? She decided she'd wait and talk with Charlie. The boy might be young but he was sensible and he'd matured a lot with his illness. Charlie often shocked her with his wisdom and she wondered how much of that was just Charlie and how much was the trauma of the last year.

Jane realized then she'd almost made up her mind. Her parents' deaths and Charlie's illness had taught her one thing, at least. You're never promised tomorrow and life was meant for living. Not running away from it.

11

"Jane! Jane wake up! Zare's here! We're going home!" Charlie bounced on Jane's bed the next morning in happiness but Jane had spent a restless night and buried her head under the covers.

"Go back to bed, child. Sissy needs her beauty rest." Her voice was muffled by the pillow.

"No, come on. Let's pack and go home. Hurry!" Charlie tickled Jane's ribs and she couldn't resist him anymore.

She pulled the boy to her and hugged him close.

"You're a terror, do you know that?" She kissed his head as she spoke, covering his face until he giggled and pulled away.

"I know but I want to go home now, Jane. It's

nice enough here but I miss Zare and Louisiana. I want to go home." He settled in her arms and looked up at the ceiling.

"That's what you really want?" She inquired, suddenly serious.

"Yes. When I get better I want to explore the swamp and learn to go out crawfishing, and to paint. I want to learn to paint the Bayou and the wildlife. And I want to do all of that with you and Zare." He looked into his sister's eyes, so like his own, and smiled sadly at her. "And you need Zare, Jane. He makes you smile so much. You haven't smiled like you smile when he's around since we left Louisiana. You need to smile like that more often and only Zare can do that."

Jane thought about his words for a moment then pushed him away.

"Alright then, sport, go get your things packed. Let me get dressed and then we'll get ready to go home."

Jane talked with Zare and they made plans to leave. They left the house around midday after Jane called the landlord and they packed up the cars. Zare promised her car would be brought back to Louisiana, along with the things she wanted to bring back that were too big or bulky to get on the plane. Then they were on the plane, speeding back to their home. Jane hoped it was the beginning of a new life. One that would have to be hidden for a little while but hopefully not for long. She needed more than a hidden life and Charlie deserved more than that. Looking over at Zare she hoped he kept his promise to keep them safe.

Jane fell asleep on the plane, somehow slept through Zare carrying her out of the plane and to the car, through the car ride home, and then into the house stealthily. It was late and the house was quiet. Jane only woke up when she felt Zare letting her down onto the bed. Jane wrapped her arms around his neck and tried to pull him close, the sensation of his body pressed to hers far too tempting.

"No, you need to be sure about that, Jane. You're still asleep." He murmured the words against her ear, his voice shaking as he spoke.

"No, stay." She urged, wrapping her legs around his waist as she moved her head to capture his lips.

She felt him relax against her body as her tongue prodded his lips and her hands pulled at the buttoned shirt he wore. She wanted nothing more in that moment than to feel his skin and when she found his warm flesh she moaned into his now open mouth. Their tongues tangled as he pressed into her, making her crave him even more.

With a sudden fierceness Zare moved, pulling her pants away as he slid his hand between her thighs, needing to touch her, to be inside of her even if it was only his fingers that got that privilege. They moved together as his fingers fucked her, his tongue teasing hers in a copycat rhythm of his fingers buried in her hot depths.

Jane broke away, her panting breaths now evident as she begged for more. Zare moved away and they each tore at their own clothes as weeks of pent up sexual frustration forced them to act quickly. Jane finished first and climbed onto Zare's lap, his pants gone but his shirt only unbuttoned. She didn't care as she sank onto his hard cock, filling herself with the long length of his thick member.

"Fuck yes!" She cried out as he stretched her depths, opening her wide for his invasion.

Her legs wrapped around his silky waist, their bodies joined tightly together as he bit into her neck and her breasts rasped against his chest hair. Zare held her hips as she rode him, letting her set the pace she needed. He was only happy to be inside of her, to be surrounded with her smooth skin and intoxicating scent once more. He could feel the pleasure building, working to a breaking point that he wouldn't let loose, not until Jane had found her own moment.

They clung together, sitting up in the bed, closer somehow than they'd ever been before as Jane moved away to stare into his eyes. Zare gasped as he watched her hazel eyes start to turn a bright yellow as her pleasure grew and her breath started to come in tiny gasps. He saw them flare into a darker shade of yellow suddenly and felt her contracting around his hardness. He lost sight of her eyes as she threw her head back in a quiet moan of drawn out pleasure.

Zare felt a powerful wave of love washing over him as he realized she truly was his mate for life now and let himself go, flooding her with his passion as they echoed their pleasure in low moans. He held her as her movements stilled, his arousal still hard within her. He didn't know how that could be but decided to take advantage of it.

He moved Jane, flipping her around so quickly it made her giggle, and found her wetness once more. He slowly slid into her, watching as her eyes closed for a moment as she took in the sensation of his entry. When she opened them once more Zare saw their yellow irises and smiled down at her. She obviously didn't know yet but he'd tell her later. For now he wanted to lose himself in her once more.

When they were done he carried Jane into the bathroom and washed her in the shower. Jane still wasn't done, however, and knelt in the spraying hot water to take him in her hand. She tasted him, clean from the shower, and sucked the head of his cock into her mouth. Zare groaned and fell back against the shower. He braced himself as he leaned into her once more, hoping she'd take him deeper into her mouth.

Jane didn't disappoint and sucked him deep down her throat, swallowing him until he felt her throat muscles massaging him. He gasped and tried not to move, wanting to let her take her time, direct what happened.

Jane felt a sense of power over him as he moaned, and even whimpered, as she sucked him, and licked him. Her tongue played along his long length, discovering every ride of his flesh once more. She loved sucking his cock and she'd missed the feel of the springy flesh of the head against her teeth. She nipped at it now and moaned in pleasure as his fingers dug into her wet hair.

With the spray of the shower pelting her face Jane went back to sucking her husband off, using her hand to masturbate him as she fucked him with her face. Her speed increased and his legs turned to stone, his stomach trembling as his pleasure grew.

"Jane, I'm going to come! I can't stop it." He ground out as she bore down on him once more, wanting him to come between her lips. She wanted to feel his hot cum in her throat, wanted to feel him pulsing against her teeth. She wanted to eat her shifter mate's seed as she sucked him deep.

Zare let her take his first few shots in her mouth but pulled away, wanting to come against her lips, to see it dripping from her mouth. He held his cock against her chin, pointing at her lips as his body jerked with each shot. Soon her lips were covered in his sperm and he smiled down into her challenging yellow eyes.

"I don't think I can do that again tonight." He said, exhaustion taking its toll.

"Oh, we can have a nap but I haven't fucked you properly for weeks now baby. You're only getting a nap!" Jane teased him as she stood up from the shower floor and wrapped herself in a towel. "I'm not nearly finished with you yet."

Zare hoped he could keep up and staggered into the bedroom with her, hoping for a few hours before she woke him up for another round.

They came out of their bedroom two days later and Jane found Charlie sitting on the couch, looking terrified and sick. Jane went to him immediately and felt his forehead. His skin was flushed and he felt warm.

"What's wrong baby boy?" She asked him.

"I'm scared, Jane. The lymph nodes under my arms are swollen again and they hurt."

Jane felt a piercing pang of terror slice through her chest. She hugged him close and realized she could smell something odd from his skin, a sick smell that made her stomach turn.

"Zare!" She called out as loud as she dared, two fears now plaguing her, why could she smell Charlie's sickness and why was he ill again?

Zare came out and knew what was up the moment he spotted Charlie and Jane's terrified faces. It was time to have a talk with them.

"Jane, Charlie, we all know what's happening here. Unfortunately I suspect this is going to keep happening. I can smell the cancer in him now too. I assume you can as well Jane?" He sat down in a chair opposite them and looked at his wife.

"Yes! Why can I smell it?" She had an idea why but wanted his confirmation.

"The baby. Sometimes human women can be turned by their unborn children. Our child will be a shifter and her blood is mixing with yours. That's turned you." He watched her face but saw only relief there.

"Well, that makes sense. So I'll be like you now?"

"Yes, and I'll teach you how to control it, what you need to do to survive, everything that goes along with it. Right now, it's important that we sort out young Charlie here." Zare looked at the boy pointedly.

"What do you mean? Change him? Charlie, do you know what that means?" Jane looked down at the young boy and knew it was a decision only he could make.

"Will I ever get sick again?" That was his first question. His only question.

"No, not like humans do. You'll never catch a human disease, or spread one, but there are some things that can make you ill. They're all things found far away from America though and we can go over those later. Right now I need to know what you want to do."

"How long will we live?" Jane interrupted.

"I'm in my 70s." Zare paused as they gasped and looked at him with new eyes. "We can live to be over 100 years old, some have lived beyond 300."

That took a moment for them to absorb but Zare saw Charlie grin before he spoke once more.

"I want to be like you." Just that quickly the boy made up his mind. He wanted far more out of life than what he was promised at the moment and Zare offered him that life. He decided to take it with both hands.

"Let me see your wrist."

Charlie held out his hand and Zare used a clean knife to make a small nick in the boys flesh. He did the same with his own wrist and held it to the child's. That easily, Charlie went from being a very ill little boy to one that was rapidly healing.

Jane was amazed to see the flush leaving Charlie's skin and a healthy glow replace it. Within an hour the boy was tearing around the apartment full of energy he hadn't had in months.

"Does this mean we're stronger too?" Charlie asked excitedly as he ran around the apartment once more.

"Yes, you'll be stronger than others your age."

"Awesome!" The boy called out as he finally settled on the couch, the burst of energy now under control. "I can help protect Jane then."

Charlie's somber words sobered them all up and they looked at each other. Their trials weren't over yet. One major hurdle had just been passed but there were still more to get through before they could all breath easily.

Zare moved over to Jane and leaned into her ear to whisper to her.

"Oh, about the birth of the baby. A lot of

human and wolf mothers find the birth of their children far unlike the birth of human children. Some even find it incredibly pleasurable."

Jane looked at him in shock but then smiled. This being a shifter thing was going to take some getting used to.

12

The hidden apartment was starting to chafe with the confinement of Charlie and Jane as months went by and the threat didn't abate. People had reacted with disbelief at the revelation of the shifter world but were now starting to accept the news as fact. This didn't stop The Faction wanting to take out Zare as the Alpha, nor did it alleviate the threat to Jane as his wife.

Zare provided for the pair well but the months flowed past, Jane's pregnancy growing daily, until she became moody and short with everybody in the hidden apartment with her. Poor Charlie couldn't escape the apartment so found ways to try to amuse her or distract her from her anger over being confined.

"Are you sure we aren't tigers, Zare?" Charlie whispered to Zare one day.

"Quite sure, Charlie, why?" Zare put down his tablet for a moment and looked at Charlie curiously.

"Because Jane's like a caged tiger, prowling around her cage." Charlie looked over at his sister, pacing between her bedroom and the living room. They both felt their eyes widen as Jane actually growled.

"Hm. Luckily, I think tonight will be the last night of your confinement. She's at the end of her rope."

"Really? We can go outside soon?" Charlie's excitement was evident in the huge grin that showcased one crooked tooth in a row of straight ones.

Zare laughed and ruffled the boy's hair. "Yes, I do believe you can. I'll be gone for the night but I'll be back tomorrow. Let me talk to your sister."

Charlie ran into his room to read a comic book while Zare talked with Jane.

"Be very careful, darling." She murmured as she cradled his head to her chest. "Take them out, but be careful."

A year ago those words would have never

passed her lips. But that was before an attempted rape, an abduction and beating, murder, and months of hiding. The reality was those people were never going to leave them in peace, leave the world in peace. They had to be dealt with.

Zare hugged his wife and left the concealment of his apartment. Many of the family and staff assumed Zare spent so much time confined in his bedroom because his wife had left him and he hadn't quite got over it. Others wondered about his disappearances but none dared disturb him when he was in his private domain. He slipped through the secret door into his room and changed his clothing, preparing for the battle to come.

He and the clan were determined to change their world, just as much as they'd changed the human world. This mission was going through with the help of several government agencies, and the illegal trade he and the family were part of had stopped. Zare no longer had to provide for hundreds of family members in hiding. They could now go out and work so there was no reason to keep up the illegal activities to provide for them. Zare was, in fact, working with the authorities to break up the supply chain.

An hour later, Zare, some of his crew, and the government task force crew were in place around a house in Houma, Louisiana, waiting to see if the leader of The Faction was in the house.

It had been agreed that none of the conspirators were going to leave the house alive. There weren't any children in the house, they'd already confirmed that, so the house was going to be demolished, the people inside obliterated. In exchange for the government cooperation Zare and his crew got out of the drug trade and turned over their contacts in Mexico.

Zare heard a faint purr, a sound not out of place in the swamp but at that pitch, it was the signal to move in and start placing the charges. Zare would have preferred taking out his enemies with his own hands but he was determined that none of the conspirators would escape. He wanted this over and done with. The fear ended tonight!

Setting the charge on one of the pylons under the house Zare stepped away stealthily, back to the cover of the cypress trees. He could see moving shadows swooping back to their spots in the swamp as he finished the countdown in his head. Brent's mother and her followers were living their last moments. A small twinge of guilt pierced at Zare's heart but he stomped it down with the image of Jane when he'd pulled her out of the room, her face broken, her body bruised, her spirit cowed. Never again.

Zare whistled low and quiet as he continued the count in his head. He reached the end of the cycle and held his breath, waiting for the moment when his world changed. The night was suddenly lit by orange flames and the shaking violence of combusting explosives.

"Fucking hell. Nobody's getting out of that alive!" Zare spoke to himself as the house was turned into splinters of wood and tiny shards of glass. Satisfaction made him hum deep in his chest. He identified the feeling as happiness.

Zare hung around long enough to ensure that all of the conspirators were somehow accounted for then went home. It was time to bring his wife and her brother out into the light, even if that was only moonlight for the moment.

He walked into the apartment and saw his wife asleep on the couch. He went into Charlie's room and saw the boy sitting on his bed, drawing a rather complicated pattern called a zentangle, and moved to get his attention.

"It's done?" Charlie asked, his young eyes far more solemn than they should be.

"Let's go outside, Charlie." Zare said with happiness and a sense of pride.

They went to the living room together and woke Jane on the couch. The months of enforced quiet and soberness were apparent as Jane and Charlie walked out quietly, not speaking, as they left the house and walked into the night.

Jane held her face up to the moonlight, inhaling the fresh scent of swamp as the wind blew gently over her body.

"Oh my. I thought I'd never feel that again." Jane placed her hand on her stomach as she enjoyed the simple peace of being outside.

"I'm sorry it took so long Jane. But it's over now. Never again will you have to hide in those rooms." Zare promised.

"Oh, I don't know, Zare. It's the perfect place to escape to isn't it?" She turned to him with a smile, her world now finally something near perfect.

"I suppose it is. Want to walk?" He looked at her with some concern, her pregnancy couldn't go on much longer and he didn't want to harm her or tire her out.

"That would be perfect, Zare." She took his arm and they walked along the driveway then down to the edge of the river. She sat on a chair on the dock and looked out over the river. Charlie's high-pitched squeal of joy as he ran along the riverbank made her heart melt. He was healthy now, a bit pale from being inside, but he was absolutely healthy now. Perfectly healthy. "Perfect."

THREE DAYS LATER JANE PRESENTED ARIELLE Loralai Mallack to the world, a beautiful little girl with her father's black eyes and her mother's beautiful grin. Jane stared down at her daughter in the bed beside her and was glad she'd chosen a home birth. She was in her home, with her family and friends, and she didn't have to listen to machines beeping.

She shifted as Dodie came in, and knocked over a dusty leather book from her nightstand. Dodie bent to pick the volume up and looked at it curiously.

"What's this?" She asked putting the volume back on the nightstand.

"It's Zare's great-grandmother's diary. She was one of the Casket Girls, the girls brought over from France as brides for the men in Louisiana. I found it just before I left the apartment. It's really enlightening and reveals some of Zare's family history."

"Wow! That is awesome! So shifter, huh? And you're one now?" Dodie asked, looking at Jane to ensure her friend was truly happy with her life.

"Yes. You keep dating that cousin of Zare's and you might be as well." Jane said, her eyes sparkling with a cheeky grin.

"You never know, huh? So much has happened this year, Jane. It's crazy, isn't it?" Dodie asked, sitting on the edge of the bed to pick up Jane's daughter.

"I almost lost hope, Dodie, I really did. You got me through the roughest part. Then Zare came along and the world just exploded. But yeah. The world is good now, for me at least."

"I'm glad I could be there for you. So, about this pleasure during birth thing?" Dodie giggled and looked at Jane with teasing glee.

"Seriously, you have to experience that, Dodie! It is the most incredible thing in the world." Jane giggled too, her cheeks turning red.

"Is it sexual?" Dodie asked, curious.

"Not really, it's just the most pleasurable, peaceful, and joyous moment of your life. I've heard horror stories about human birth and some really great stories about how awesome it is, but I wouldn't change my experience for anything.

"Perfect, was it?" Dodie cooed at Arielle as Jane watched them with satisfaction.

"Like most things lately, it was downright perfect."

The End

EXTENDED EPILOGUE - SOLD TO THE WEREWOLF

"Here, Dodie." Jane handed a folder to her friend, noting the other woman's confusion with a smile.

"What's this?" the other woman asked, flipping through the pages.

"You remember that diary of Zare's great-grandmother? You couldn't read it because it was in French, I translated it for you."

"Good grief, Jane, that was over a year ago!" Dodie sat down in a chair in Jane's living room, on the "right side of the bayou", and gave her friend a pleased smile. "I just, how long did this take you?"

Dodie's brows knitted together, perfect arches over her eyes.

"Well, I started after the baby was born and

finished it a couple of weeks ago. So, almost a year. I wanted to give it to you then, but as you'll be part of the family tomorrow, well, I thought it might make a nice wedding present." Jane sat in a chair of her own, patting her rounded belly. Baby number two was on the way.

"This is too much, Jane! It's four inches thick!" She looked at the folder incredulously.

Jane gave her a soothing smile, waving Dodie's protests away. "It was a pleasure to do. Zare's going to have it published for the family too."

Jane looked pleased, so Dodie stopped her protesting and took the gift for what it was.

"Thank you, Jane, and thank you for everything else."

"Well, you wanted to marry that woman of yours so I made arrangements for it. Whose business is it, anyway?" They were all flying to California in an hour on Zare's private jet.

"I just can't believe I'm lucky enough to have a friend like you." Dodie sat back, thinking over their friendship.

"You did the same for me, Dodie, and still do. Now, let's get on that plane!" Jane pulled her friend out of the chair and they were soon sitting comfortably in the small jet. Dodie took out the book Jane had given her and began to read as everyone settled down after take-off. Jane was asleep, Charlie was reading a comic, and Zare was doing something with his tablet.

Dodie's bride was already in California, waiting on her as was the rest of the wedding party. Tomorrow was the big day and she couldn't settle because of her excitement. She wasn't nervous, she was excited for the rest of her life to start.

Settling in, she opened to the first page.

December 25th, 1728

New Orleans, Louisiana Territory

My name is Angelique Therese Burelle, and I am one lucky young woman. I was seventeen years old when I came to this tropical hell on earth. The government sold it to us as a paradise, a place of fruits and honey, and also a place where a lady could find a husband. As an orphan, I agreed to take the journey to the New World, to this

Louisiana Territory, and hoped I could make a new life for myself.

I cannot say that I live in paradise, not with the heat and humidity, those awful hurricanes that creep upon us with such devastation, and those rather horrid mosquito, not to mention the disease! Yellow fever, scarlet fever, diphtheria, consumption, and something the locals call swamp fever are all rife here. Life is not easy in this territory, not easy at all, and many succumb to any number of ills, or the wildlife! My God, the snakes, some large reptile called an alligator, and any number of other wild creatures can leap out of nowhere at any given moment and kill you! I've even heard there are wolves in the area now.

Of course, the city isn't that old by most standards, and we have to do without many things here. Cheese spoils before one can even get it home, if one is lucky enough to find some, and meat is often found to be rancid. What I would not give for a nice loaf of bread from a bakery at home! Alas, I will not be going back to France, for I am married and with child now. At 18 I am a married woman with a husband that owns a large estate, though it isn't much of an estate yet. There is a lot of swamp to be drained and cleared, but my husband, Gilbert Mallack, had plans and the labor force to help.

He gave me this diary as he knows I am lonely, with friends so far and few in between. I shall write more when I need to the most. Paper is even a precious commodity here and must be kept safe from the damp. I shall do my best.

Dodie saw that the next few entries concerned the birth of Angelique's child, then children, and flipped through until she saw the notation of the death of a child. A fever took the little girl in the night and the poor young woman was devastated, writing that even moving into their new grand house with the mosquito netting hadn't prevented the girl's fever and subsequent death. Dodie's heart broke for Angelique but she kept reading. She soon learned that Angelique had birthed 13 children, 8 of those lived to start their own families.

Dodie glanced at Zare, knowing that it was his grandfather who became the first wolf shifter in his family and that Zare, though he looked nothing like it, was over 70 years old. He was the product of this young woman Dodie was dreaming about. She found it utterly amazing.

June 08, 1748

For almost 20 years I have walked the dangers of this wretched place, courting danger in places that even the most defenseless should normally feel safe. There are a thousand ways to die in this plagued land and tonight, my son Etienne faced a danger many of us had thought was gone. He was attacked by a wolf and fights for his very life. I am not at all sure it is a battle he will win.

...

Etienne yet lives. A week has passed and his chest still rises and falls. For a while, we thought it was done, that he would close his eyes for the last time, but he is recovering now. May God bless him and see him through this.

...

It has been a month. A lot has changed. Things I dare not speak about. Things I almost dare not write about. All those years ago, Gilbert gave me this book to ease my loneliness and never have I needed it more than I do now. My son is some kind of beast! He has attacked his entire family and now they are also this same kind of beast! We know not what to do with him, other than to protect him, and his family, from those that might destroy them. How can it be? Oh, my sweet Jesus, how can this be?

Dodie looked up as the plane ran into a bit of turbulence, before going back to the pages. There were records of more births, a few deaths of the elderly, a few accidents, but no more deaths due to illness. The entire family, it seemed, was incredibly resistant to the diseases now and the neighbors were starting to take notice.

December 25th, 1778

War. The men still go on about war. America has declared itself free of Britain and has now won the war to prove it. Why do they still go on about war? We aren't even a part of America, yet the men...

Oh, it's just too tedious and I am too old. I have been in this land for 50 years now and I tell you, I'm ready to lay down and let it all go. I have lost five children, seen poverty that is unimaginable, been an orphan, sailed from one country across a great ocean to another, I have learned how to be a plantation wife, how to care for children, and how to nurse the dying.

I have also seen my children and grandchildren become beasts of unimaginable horror. Each one has had to leave their home for decades because they do not age as normal humans do. I spent 20 years without seeing them. I suppose I'll be dead before they come home again.

My life has not been easy, not at all, and I've had to carry a much heavier burden than many. I do not begrudge the Lord my life, however. I may have a long list of complaints, but I know that my children will have long lives, even if they did take a few lives in the earliest days of their own burdens.

They are my children, though, and I love them. I learned to love their father, may he rest in peace, these last two years, but my children I love without reserve. I know that there are many that would see them slaughtered but I cannot allow that. I have protected them for this long, I will not reveal the shame that has befallen our family now. Their father's plantation sustains them, and soon Etienne will return to take the reins.

My son, my eldest and strongest son, has offered me the life he leads. He says that the burden will take away the pain of my aching joints, that it will relieve the mysterious sensation I feel in the missing fingers of my left hand, fingers I lost while working to prepare the sugar cane for processing. Fingers that I can still feel moving.

I appreciate his feelings on the matter, and know that he likely does not want to face losing his mother as well, but my time on this earth is nearly done and I could not be happier about it.

What mother wants her child to be a murderer, what mother could live with that knowledge? I have for a long time, recriminating myself often, but I could not do anything to relieve myself of that. Etienne did not choose to be attacked, nor did he choose to be a murderer. It was forced on him, as he forced it on others in our family when he'd shifted into his wolf form. He had no control and had to learn, as the others had to learn.

...

I could not finish that last entry, my heartache grew too much to endure. A week has passed and I am full of cold, with a fire in my chest that cannot be put out. Coughing wracks my frail body, a body that once attracted the gaze of a rich man, but is now old and stooped. I learned to read and write in that French convent all those decades ago and I now suppose that this will be the last time I use such a talent.

Etienne returned today, looking no older than the last time I saw him. My child, my beautiful boy, is a demon. I want you to know, though, my dear son, I want all of my dear children to know, that if they ever read this, they are not to think that I did not love them. I loved all of my children, and that love will spread throughout eternity. I hope one day we shall meet again, perhaps in another life, or another world.

I do not think the Lord will allow you into a realm such as His, so I have not repented my final sins, so that I may meet you in whatever punishment awaits all sinners.

A note from Jane Mallack (translator)

There are no entries after this point, and later record searches showed that Angelique died the night she wrote that last entry. She was a brave woman, obviously full of life and spirit, and most importantly, she was full of love. I think that is a lesson that all in our family, blood-born, adopted, turned, or married family members should work to emulate. Love got Angelique through the hardest times in her life, she would not want what the future has wrought, cousin fighting cousin. Think about that, think about who you are now, and know, that you are a part of Angelique, and she faced eternal damnation out of love for us all.

Dodie closed the book, knowing she would go over it more thoroughly at a later date, but now she knew what she was stepping into with this marriage. A family founded on love, that was facing a new future full of peace. Not too shabby. She sat back in her seat and smiled, holding the massive diary to her chest. Not too shabby at all for a woman from the wrong side of the bayou.

ACKNOWLEDGMENTS

I would like to thank my editor Caroline and my publisher Lovy Books, who have been of huge support to me during the writing of this book.

Special thanks to my lovely street team: Pat Boggie, Darlene Dupee, Faraona del sol, Nessa, Sue Hutchings, Monica Woodmansee, Patricia Hoffstaetter, Connie Grove, Linda, Bea Leija, Darcy Smith and those who wish to remain anonymous.

SUMMER COOPER

DISCOVER THE WILD GIRL IN YOU

Besides her love of chocolate, dogs and music... reading and writing is Summer's number one route to escape from crazy friends, family and the in-laws!

She found her own happily ever after with a martial arts fighter who also happens to be an adorable IT geek! Now, she loves to write about hot alpha males that come with a pretty face and covered in tough-as-nails muscle... who are secretly looking for their true soul mate (shhh...)!

If you wish to get in touch, please email her at hello@summercooper.com and she'll get back to you as soon as she can.